Hidden Kingdom

Rise of the Giants Series: Book 5

Theo Mann

The Invisible Publishing Company

Rise of the Giants Series

Contents

Chapter 1

M ora paused to heft the bundle in her arms, but nothing could make it more comfortable. Her arms strained to the breaking point and the weight made her back ache.

She only gave herself a few seconds to stop before she pushed herself to keep going. The bundle in her arms squirmed when she tried to adjust its position. She looked down at her baby daughter Anava curled up in the wrap tied around Mora's chest.

"I'm tired, Mother," her three-year-old son Maeno complained.

Mora squeezed his hand. "I'm tired, too, my love. I'm really tired. Sometimes I get so tired I don't think I can go another step."

"Why haven't we gotten to the gorges yet?" seven-year-old Zaedi asked from behind Mora's back. "Shadow and Father made it sound like they were right around the corner from our old camp."

"You know as much as I do, my son," Mora told him. "You've heard your father talking. The band has had to divert into multiple alternate courses to avoid enemy Clans—not to mention dangerous creatures."

Zaedi squinted up at the sky. "It will be dark soon. We should be stopping to camp."

"I highly doubt Shadow will stop the band here," Mora returned. "We would be exposed to attacks here."

Her children didn't answer. They didn't usually complain about the hardships on the journey. Shadow's band of Godless wasn't even heading for their gorge camp anymore.

Shadow didn't announce to the band where he planned to take everyone for shelter against the enemy Clans invading from the west. He might have told Hangman and the other men if he had any plan at all. Shadow didn't tell the women anything.

A long, single-file line of people wound ahead of and behind Mora's family. The band traveled through these steep, rocky cliffs and passes much more quickly than Hangman's band had traveled to the north country.

This was a far more dangerous country to travel through than those rugged mountains. The men couldn't climb up the cliffs to search the countryside for any sign of danger.

The men had to travel right in the middle of the line. The path only offered a few feet of space for the people to pass one or two at a time.

A vertical stone wall rose on Mora's left as high as the stark blue sky overhead. Another wall dropped straight down on her right and plunged thousands of feet into the gorge below.

The only good thing about this journey was that no enemy Clans could strike the band from any direction—not without everyone in the band seeing them coming.

Shadow, Hangman, Viking, Red, and Wildling led the party at the front in case anyone came at the band from that direction.

Any enemy Clan who did attack from the front could only come one man at a time, too. They wouldn't be able to get to the women and children in the center of the group.

Prodigy, Bantam, Devil, Grizzly, and Breaker brought up the rear for the same reason. The rest of the men and uninitiated boys spread themselves through the rest of the band.

The band had suffered a catastrophic blow when Hammer left with his whole party and taken Cross with him. They had left Shadow's band sorely lacking in fighting men.

The uninitiated boys had to step in while the freed captives from the Bounty Hunters' village did their best to fill the gaps. Shadow didn't approve of outsiders and uninitiated boys fighting with initiated Godless men, but he had no choice but to accept the new situation.

Hangman, Viking, Red, and all of Red's men had been doing it Hangman's way for so long that they adapted easily. The men welcomed the uninitiated boys of Shadow's band with open arms.

Red and his men had started training the boys right away, encouraging them to rise to the challenge, and giving them tips and suggestions on how to improve. Bantam was still young enough to understand the need of this and joined right in.

He had taken his youngest brother Jerun under his wing. Bantam had made it his mission to give Jerun all the help he could possibly want and need. The boys thrived with this new support they had never gotten from Shadow or his men.

Shadow resented this and it made him surly. He didn't outright speak against the changes. He couldn't. He needed Hangman and his men too much to protect the band.

Anyone could see Shadow simmering with barely suppressed fury that someone was acting against his wishes. He answered curtly whenever someone spoke to him.

Sometimes he absolutely refused even to look at the uninitiated boys, including his own son, or the men who trained them.

The fighting men who had been with Shadow all this time also saw the writing on the wall.

Banjo and Feather fell right back into their old habit of deferring decision-making to Hangman. They obeyed him instantly unless Shadow had already given them some instructions to the contrary.

Devil, Breaker, and Grizzly didn't warm to Hangman as quickly, but they couldn't deny his authority. They didn't obey him and they didn't disobey him.

They didn't shy away from accepting the uninitiated boys, either. The three brothers just went along with whatever the other men did.

Mora did her best not to pay too much attention to what the men did. They had to work it out between themselves. She still found herself counting up the men she knew would back Hangman if Shadow really decided to push his authority too far.

She didn't have to worry about Red's men. They all obeyed Hangman to the letter. They only subordinated themselves to Shadow because Hangman did it.

Red and his men would have split from Shadow in an instant if Hangman told them to. Red and his men would have thought nothing of taking their wives and children and leaving the rest of Shadow's band twisting in the wind.

Mora had spent too many years living with these men not to understand their facial expressions and body language. She saw plenty of Red's men grimacing in annoyance behind Shadow's back.

They didn't like him and they especially didn't appreciate his attitude toward Hangman. Red and his men blamed Shadow for driving Hammer away and putting the whole band in danger in the process.

The rift between Shadow and Hangman still had not recovered in the last three years since the two bands joined. Only Hangman's constant deference and conciliation prevented an outright rift between him and his father.

Mora took a second to hitch Anava a little higher in the wrap. Mora needed to retie it to make it tighter against her body, but she couldn't take the time to do it now.

Anava stayed permanently latched onto Mora's breast. Mora had to support Anava's weight in her arms until the band's next break.

Shadow didn't take breaks the way Hangman used to. Shadow pretended not to notice pregnant women, mothers, and their young children struggling to keep up. He never once turned around to check how the rest of the band was doing.

His attitude turned the men of Hangman's former band against Shadow more than anything. Viking and Red's men especially stopped many times a day to help people who simply could not keep up and fell behind or collapsed.

Viking, Rapid, and Legend had even been known to pick up pregnant women and carry them until Shadow decided to stop for the night. Quite a few of the men carried their younger children piggyback to take the pressure off the mothers.

Their actions infuriated Shadow, but he never said a word about it to anyone when he bothered to notice it at all. He buried all that resentment inside himself. He outright glared at people, but he never actually came right out and told anyone not to.

The men did it more and more often just to spite him. Mora could just see these men counting down the seconds before one of them had to stand up to him and point out that he couldn't reasonably expect them to leave pregnant women and little children behind to perish.

The confrontation was bound to come sooner or later, but it still hadn't come after three years of traveling. The tension kept rising.

Mora always made sure to keep up and to take care of her children no matter how tired she got. Hangman couldn't afford to be the spark that set fire to Shadow's fuse.

Hangman had become progressively more silent as the months dragged on. He rarely spoke about anything whenever there was the slightest chance that Shadow might hear.

He spoke the same as ever when his father wasn't around. The men all deferred to Hangman whenever they got separated from Shadow. Then Hangman fell silent again as soon as his father came around.

Hangman's silence only seemed to harden Shadow against Hangman even more. Shadow seemed to suspect Hangman of plotting against him in secret, but the subject never came out into open conflict. Both men left it alone and so did everyone else.

Mora caught sight of them every now and then when the path turned a corner around some ledge. Shadow led the band at the very front of the line. Hangman had positioned himself behind Viking so Viking would separate Hangman from his father.

Red and Wilding walked behind Hangman to keep as much distance between themselves and Shadow as possible. Shadow would have had to be blind not to see the way the men acted toward him.

Mora sighed and hitched Anava up again, but a high-pitched shriek startled the whole band to high alert right then.

Human attackers couldn't threaten the band on these cliffs, but the position left them exposed to creatures attacking from the air. Ridgebeaks and Boultars patrolled these canyons. Airborne creatures could spot exposed people a long way off.

The narrow path left women and children defenseless. The men couldn't protect everyone. The men also couldn't band together to fight a full-sized Ridgebeak if one did attack.

"Run!" Viking roared over his shoulder. "MOVE!!"

The whole band burst into a run including children who had been dragging their heels just a few minutes ago. Mora grabbed Maeno's hand on one side and Thena's on the other side, but no one could run any faster than the people in front of them.

Shadow, Viking, Hangman, Red, and Wildling outpaced everyone, raced ahead, and dove into a channel cutting between the steep cliffs. These channels offered the only protection from attacking creatures.

The women and children dove into the channel behind the men. The channel widened where water had washed out the rock and created a wider place. It gave a tiny, sheltered place for the women and children to take cover from the assault.

The party streamed ahead much faster as more and more people made it to the channel. Mora shoved her children in there. The men and uninitiated boys fell in ranks with Shadow and the others as they all made it to that one spot.

The five men drew their weapons and Wildling unwound the rope from his waist. He never went anywhere without it. The men rotated outward to face the incoming threat. Mora didn't need to see what it was.

This was the one critical disadvantage of traveling through the gorges. No one could see a creature attacking from the air until it came within a dozen yards of actually snatching someone.

The Ridgebeaks and Boultars had learned this strategy. They always attacked from behind the cliffs. No one in the band could see the creatures coming until the last possible second. The men looked all around them, but the Ridgebeak still didn't show itself.

More women and children dove into the channel and more men surrounded it. Mora and the others had to smash themselves inside so everyone could fit.

Half the band got there in time. Prodigy, Bantam, and the other men still trapped in and behind the band turned outward. The Ridgebeak could only attack from that direction.

Mora heard the men yelling, but she couldn't hear what they were saying over the noise of all the other voices in the channel. Women called to their children to get down and stay down. Mothers clasped their children tighter to stop anyone from running away in panic.

The last members of the band raced up the path, and at that moment, a massive male Ridgebeak swooped around a corner of a different cliff behind the fleeing Godless.

Prodigy and the others raised their weapons, but the Ridgebeak knew better than to go near the men. The creature angled its wings and swerved at the last second, stalled over the bottom gorge, and adjusted its momentum to come at the band from out in open space.

The men spun around and rushed the women and children to surround them, but not fast enough. The Ridgebeak's speed carried it forward and it snatched one of the freed captives from the Bounty Hunters' village.

The woman screamed and fought back. Bantam lunged for her and brought his kukri down hard on the Ridgebeak's foot. The bird shrieked in fury and clubbed him with its wing. He stumbled, but he didn't fall. He tried one last time to grab the woman and pull her back.

The Ridgebeak pumped its wings in one powerful beat of rushing wind and pulled the woman over the side just as the other men charged in to attack.

The bird retreated too fast and yanked Bantam over the side at the same time. The woman screamed one last time before she fell out of sight.

Hangman surged out of line and roared, "BANTAM!"

He would have rushed over there to save his brother, but Shadow grabbed Hangman by the shoulder and pulled him back. Prodigy got there a second later and grabbed Bantam by the wrist just as gravity threatened to snatch him down into the plunging gorge.

Bantam dropped his kukri in a frantic effort to grab Prodigy's hand. Bantam's weight would have pulled Prodigy to his death, too, but Devil, Grizzly, and Breaker got there first.

They seized Prodigy by his loincloth, and when that failed, they held him back by his legs and feet.

The three brothers flattened themselves to the ground and held on to stop both men from falling over the side.

Hangman shook off his father's hand and sprinted back down the path. Viking and Legend went with him.

Viking and Legend were two of the biggest, strongest men in the band. Grizzly was the other. Grizzly couldn't let go of Prodigy's legs long enough to help pull the men up.

Viking, Legend, and Hangman had to lie down on top of Prodigy and Breaker to get hold of Bantam. The men hauled him up and he collapsed panting and gasping on the ground while they pulled up Prodigy next.

None of the men moved for a second. It was a miracle the band had only lost one person that time. They had lost more in similar attacks.

The men took a long time to pick themselves up and limp back up the path to rejoin the rest of the band. Shadow only glared at them—especially Hangman.

Hangman didn't make eye contact with his father. Hangman paid attention only to Bantam and the others. He went from man to man making sure none of them had gotten hurt.

Shadow finally turned around and surveyed the women and children hiding in the channel. "It's getting dark," he growled. "We'll camp here tonight and push on in the morning."

Chapter 2

Hangman sat down next to Mora and the children. Wildling and his wife and children sat nearby. Mora pulled some dried food out of her band and handed one piece each to her three children.

"You missed that one, Wildling," she told him. "Better luck next time."

"I wouldn't try to catch a Ridgebeak on one of those narrow paths," he replied. "That would be the quickest way to get myself killed."

"What about laying a trap for one right outside this channel?" Mora asked. "Is that enough open ground for you to do it?"

"Sure," Wildling replied. "Just get Prodigy, Rapid, Butch, and Legend to lie in wait with their ropes to bring the bird down."

"We can't do it here," Hangman pointed out. "We don't have any firewood to cook and cure the meat. It would all go to waste. Wait until we get somewhere with trees."

Wildling didn't answer. He turned away to take care of his family. The band was getting dangerously low on food. The party had encountered the same problem everywhere they went in these canyons.

Hangman kicked himself for opening his mouth. Even now, he sensed Shadow's eyes burning into Hangman's head from behind.

Hangman shouldn't have made a suggestion that one of the men could interpret as a decision. Hangman couldn't voice his opinion without his father acting like Hangman was taking some authority in this band.

He had started to wonder lately if he had made a colossal mistake by bringing his people back to Shadow's band.

Hangman had considered more than once during the last three years if he should split from Shadow, take anyone who would go with him, and trek back to their own country. He might be able to catch up with Hammer's band after all.

Hangman couldn't do that now. The band had traveled too far away. Such a small band wouldn't survive on its own. Neither band would survive if they split up the fighting men now.

Katha would stay with Shadow. Hangman couldn't bear to leave her—or to ask Jerun and Bantam to leave her. Their family had already lost Cross.

Mora distracted Hangman by bumping his arm. She handed him the largest piece of dried food she had in her bag and started chewing a much smaller piece for herself.

"Thank you," he murmured.

She gave him a look overflowing with understanding. She didn't have to say she understood the impossible mess in which he found himself. She saw it all as plain as day.

The men all saw it, too. The hostility between Shadow and Hangman was bound to come to a head sooner or later.

Hangman really hoped Shadow didn't wind up challenging Hangman in front of the whole band. Hangman didn't want to get into a situation where he had to kill his own father just to save his life and his wife's and children's lives.

Hangman would never challenge Shadow no matter how much Shadow hated him. Hangman could see some of the other men winding up to do it, though. Some of the men spoke up plainly if they disagreed with Shadow's decisions. No Kral could tolerate that.

The longer Shadow did tolerate it, the more likely it would end in a challenge on one side or the other. Then Hangman would become Kral.

That was the thing Shadow most feared—that Hangman would use the men's allegiance to unseat Shadow and make Hangman their Kral in his place.

All the men wanted that. Hangman would have given anything to go back to being on friendly terms with Shadow. Hangman just didn't see any way to avoid the conflict turning to bloodshed.

The bad blood had all started with Hammer leaving. Shadow had never recovered from that. He just would not believe that a man as young as Hammer could be Kral in his own right. Even Red and his men understood that.

A drumming sound got everyone's attention just then. The first sprinkles of rain pattered into the channel. Heavy clouds moved over the gorge country and brought darkness sooner than usual.

The women and children shrank against the walls for protection as the rain got stronger. The men sat on the outside. There wasn't enough room under the channel's curving side walls to shelter everyone.

Hangman crowded in to block Maeno and Thena from the rain. It built into a downpour. The trickle of water running through the bottom of the channel got bigger. It swelled into a stream.

Shadow stood up. "We should move out of this channel before the water gets any higher. Come on. Let's continue to another sheltered place. The creatures won't attack us in the rain."

"We can't go now," Jolt countered. "It's too dark out there."

Shadow glared at him. "I said get up and move. We're leaving."

He strode out onto the path and turned right to continue in the direction the band had been going before. Hangman stood up and picked up Maeno in his arms. The little boy was already starting to whimper in protest that he had to travel some more at this time of night.

Hangman heard muttering in the background. Some of the families didn't get up at all.

"The water is getting higher," Hangman told them. "It will fill this channel soon anyway. Come on. We have to go."

Mora got to her feet and Wildling helped his family move out. Mora picked up Thena and carried her on the other side of Anava's wrap. Hangman walked out of the channel into the pounding rain. It drenched everyone the minute they set foot outside.

He stayed there in the channel to make sure everyone got out. The pelting rain fed the stream even more. No one could sit on the floor anymore without getting wet. The band had to leave.

Mora couldn't carry Thena and Anava at the same time, so Mora put Thena down and took the girl's hand. Zaedi followed her and held onto one of her shoulder bags. Hangman decided to bring up the rear so he wouldn't have to walk near Shadow.

Maybe it would be better for Hangman to leave than to risk getting into a challenge with Shadow. Hangman took that risk every day he stayed with Shadow.

On the other hand, maybe Hangman should just outright challenge Shadow and get it over with. Hangman already knew he could beat Shadow in a fight and all the men would follow Hangman if it came to that.

He pushed that thought out of his mind, but it kept coming back no matter how much he tried to squash it.

Mora and the children walked off into the darkness to follow the path. Traveling in the rain and the dark would be much more dangerous than creatures attacking. This wouldn't be the first time Hangman disagreed with one of Shadow's decisions.

The safety and protection of his people trumped every other consideration. Hangman had learned that the hard way during his years as Kral of his own band.

He just could not justify putting the safety of the band ahead of allegiance to his father—or any other Kral. No man deserved to be Kral if he didn't protect the band. Putting the band in danger automatically disqualified a man from being Kral.

Hangman knew it. All of Red's men knew it. Even Shadow's men knew it.

Hangman should have challenged Shadow a long time ago on that alone. Hangman's own attachment and care for his father stopped him.

That was not the behavior of any decent Kral. Hangman shouldn't show mercy to any man who put the band in danger, even if that man was his own father.

Hangman couldn't do anything about that right now—not in this darkness. The Godless had to walk right up against the cliff wall to avoid stumbling too close to the edge in the dark and falling over the side.

Mora and the children had been among the first to leave the channel to follow Shadow. They wound up at the front of the line.

Hangman found himself near the middle, but he caught occasional glimpses of them farther ahead. They were all right up there.

Helping everyone distracted him. He didn't check on his family for another half an hour. When he looked up, he spotted Shadow, Katha,

Mora, the children, and a few others standing in front of a different channel. This one was empty.

Rain hammered down on everyone and stung Hangman's skin. He would have suggested to Shadow that the band take shelter in this new channel—or just about anywhere other than walking around in the rain and the dark.

Hangman didn't suggest that. He was still forty yards away helping another mother with her young children, but he wouldn't have suggested it even if he'd been standing right there next to his father. This situation couldn't go on this way. It was untenable.

He resigned himself to keep on walking all night if necessary—unless one of the other men challenged Shadow right this very minute. Hangman really wouldn't have been at all surprised.

He and those near him drew level with the channel. The smaller children took their time climbing down the slippery rock to join with the others. A gap had developed between the people already here and those who had delayed leaving the first channel. They lagged behind.

Shadow grimaced at them, turned away, and said, "Let's go."

He started climbing up the path on the other side. A few different men exchanged glances with Hangman, but no one opened their mouths to contradict—not yet.

The people gathered here struggled up the other slope to follow Shadow. Hangman went back to helping the children. Mora started to follow Shadow, too, but right then, Maeno started crying. Hangman didn't see why.

Maeno stretched out his arms to Mora. Hangman put him down on the ground so the boy could go to her. She squatted down in front of Maeno to take care of whatever it was that he needed.

Hangman concentrated on the other nearby children. He had to lift some of them and put them higher up the slope so they didn't slip down. He started to climb up after them and turned around to see if Mora needed help.

She saw him, stood up, and turned around to lead the children after him. She made eye contact with him and made a face of mock annoyance at another delay.

At that moment, a massive cascade of water crashed down the channel from somewhere higher up the cliffs.

The constant drum of rainfall masked the sound of the flood coming closer. Hangman didn't see or hear it until the moment it slammed into the channel walls.

The torrent hit the walls coming around a curve, churned over on itself, and smashed into Mora and all four children from the side.

"MORA!!" Hangman bellowed, but it was too late. The flood erased her and all four 6

His stomach plummeted into his shoes. He froze and stared at the place where his family had just been standing. They all vanished in the blink of an eye.

Nothing remained but a wall of water blocking the channel. All the people trailing behind had to stop there. They couldn't cross to rejoin the rest of the band.

Some of the men in front of Hangman must have told Shadow what was going on. Hangman was still standing there in stunned shock when his father came back down the hill and stopped there to stare at the flood, too.

Everyone else in the band stood on the other side staring across. No one could get through that.

Drilling rain stabbed all its needle pricks into Hangman's skin, but he couldn't feel a thing. His family couldn't be gone. They just couldn't be. His mind refused to accept it.

He had seen the devastating effects on his men when they thought they'd lost their wives and children. He couldn't go through that. He couldn't face a single night without them—or at least knowing they were there.

Seven years. Seven years of bliss. That's what he got. He absolutely would not go back to being alone. He would rather die first.

"I guess we have to stop here," Shadow growled. "We'll have to find a sheltered place for the rain to stop."

Hangman turned away and started hiking up the hill heading off in the direction Shadow had been going to begin with.

"Where are you going?" Shadow yelled after him. "I said we're stopping here."

"I'm going to find Mora and the children."

"Hey!" Shadow bellowed. "Come back here!"

Hangman didn't listen. He kept going. Mora and the children weren't here. He had to find them even if it cost his life.

Chapter 3

Catastrophic forces punched Mora in all directions. They tumbled her over and over in the water, threw her out just long enough for her to snatch a breath of air, and pulled her under again to slam her against hard objects rumbling and churning in the flood.

She fell over some kind of waterfall, smashed down hard on what felt like solid stone, and the force of her fall plunged her deep into another churning mass of water.

Tree limbs, boulders, and what felt like bodies pummeled her beneath the surface. She fought to struggle out of the torrent to find some air somewhere. Her head emerged in pitch darkness.

She barely filled her lungs before another brutal smash of overpowering water slammed her from the side and tore her under again. The sheering force of multiple torrents hitting each other ripped the wrap off her body.

Mora tried to grab Anava, but the wrap bundle vanished into the darkness before Mora got her arms around it to hold it back.

Another bone-crushing force hurled her away, bowled her over and over, slammed her down on the rocky streambed below her, and something very hard hit her in the head and knocked her out.

She came to her senses lying half-submerged in water up to her chest. She floundered to lift her head and looked around her in mounting horror.

She lay on a gravel bar somewhere in the deepest jungle. She had absolutely no idea where she was or where Shadow's band was.

She pried her face out of the gravel and winced. Scrapes, cuts, and bruises covered her all over her body. At least she didn't have any broken bones.

She groaned in agony and pushed herself up onto her hands and knees. She didn't see any sign of her children—especially Anava. The baby couldn't have survived that flood.

None of her children could have survived it. Maeno was only three and none of the three older children knew how to swim.

She staggered to her feet and looked around everywhere. She was all alone here. Water saturated her hair and clothes.

Her two Renegade blades hung from their knots at the waistband of her loincloth. They had come out of their sheaths in the flood, but at least she still had them. She would be able to hunt and defend herself with them.

She put them back in their sheaths so she could move around. She also still had her shoulder bags, but she didn't have any food. She would need to hunt soon.

She limped up the gravel bar and stopped at the edge of the trees. Where exactly should she go?

The water that had swept her away kept churning down the streambed next to her. The gravel bar had saved her life. She would have kept rushing down that channel forever if the water hadn't flown over the gravel bar just there.

Her children might have washed away downstream. They could be miles away from here if they were still alive at all. She couldn't go upstream and downstream at the same time. She had to choose. The band was upstream, so she went that way.

She hobbled in a stoop and pressed her bruised arms close to her body. She didn't want to move at all, but she had to go somewhere. She couldn't stay here.

She didn't know how she could ever rejoin Shadow's band. She might by some miracle have been able to climb back up all the mountains and waterfalls to the place where she and the children had gotten swept away.

Shadow's band wouldn't be there anymore. They would have moved on. It might take her years just to make it back to that one spot. The band would be long gone.

She followed the riverbed. She had no idea if it would lead back to the same channel. She could only hope.

One person traveling alone in the jungle was a death sentence—unless the person was a powerful warrior like Hangman or one of his cousins. She wasn't a powerful warrior like them. She wouldn't survive out here, especially not if she was injured.

She needed food and a place to rest. She needed to take some time to heal her injuries—but she still needed to hunt. She decided to use some of the Followers' trapping methods instead. They would be safer and less likely to get her further injured or killed.

She had come to her senses on the gravel bar around noon. She walked for an hour before hunger and exhaustion caught up with her. She had to get something to eat soon before she lost her strength to go on.

She slumped at the base of a tree, rested her head back against the trunk, and shut her eyes while she thought it over. Some creature was bound to come out of the jungle to hunt her eventually.

She just hoped whatever creature it was would be something small enough for her to kill and butcher by herself.

She checked her injuries. She should make leaf paste for them, but she didn't have the strength to do that now. She decided to rest at least until the end of the day, but hunger drove her to her feet.

She continued for another hour before she heard a Gurlg scratching in the undergrowth. She turned off to her right to find out where the creature was. A Gurlg was too big for just one person, but it was better than nothing.

She found the bird pecking in an open place against another rock wall. The bird squawked a few times, darted its beak toward the ground, and slammed its beak into a corner where the rock face embedded itself in the soil.

A child's screech split the usual jungle noise. That sound set all of Mora's hair on end. It was Maeno's voice. Then she heard Thena crying in terror.

Mora sprang out of hiding behind the Gurlg. This one was a big male—bigger than any Gurlg she had ever faced before.

The bird didn't see her, but she saw her two younger children. They had taken shelter in a hollow at the base of the rock. The cramped space barely gave them enough room to crouch in there with their arms around each other.

Maeno screamed every time the Gurlg tried to dart its beak down to snap the two children out of their hiding place.

Thena held onto her little brother and bawled her eyes out in petrified horror. The Gurlg's giant head blocked the children from seeing anything beyond its enormous eye staring at them. Mora only saw them when the Gurlg moved its head out of the way.

She snatched her blades out of their sheaths, charged up behind the Gurlg, and hacked it across the back of the leg right above the ankle joint. The joint stood as high as her head and angled backward from the place where the leg joined up with the bird's body.

The bird spun around in a heartbeat, lunged for her, and collapsed on its injured leg. The Gurlg hit the dirt and Mora charged the creature while it flopped and struggled to right itself.

Protective fury for her children gave her all the energy she needed. She didn't feel her injuries anymore. She dove for the Gurlg, dodged its beak when it tried to snap at her, and pivoted inside the radius of the bird's neck.

She slammed her body against the creature's neck to push its head away and hacked her blade across the side of the neck to take the Gurlg down.

The Gurlg choked when it tried to both squawk, breathe, and snap its beak at the same time. The creature struggled to get up again and flopped the other way.

Its thrashing almost crushed Mora. She had to leap out of the way, but it was all over. The Gurlg flapped its wings, raised its head, and slammed down in its death throes. Blood poured from the wound in its neck and got all over the Gurlg's feathers.

Mora paced around the creature watching for an opening, but she couldn't get near it until it stopped thrashing around so much.

It kept flapping its wings and lumbering over and over in different directions trying to change its position before it crashed down into the dirt for the last time.

Chapter 4

Mora couldn't get near the hollow to retrieve her children. She had to wait for the Gurlg to completely collapse. It started twitching. That's when the two children saw her. "MOTHER!!" Thena screamed.

Mora strode around the bird and paused again just to make sure it wouldn't rise again to attack her. She waited a few more minutes until the twitching stopped. The creature stopped moving completely.

She hustled the rest of the way to the hollow and extended her arms inside. "I'm here, my loves. I'm here. Come on out. You're safe. The Gurlg is dead. You're safe. You can come out now."

The children broke down in full hysterical sobbing, screaming, and bellowing when they saw her. They completely forgot to come out of the hollow. She had to pry them out by main force.

Both of them strapped themselves around her the minute she got them free. They crushed her in their arms sobbing their eyes out. She didn't try to take them off. She didn't want to stop holding them.

She had them back. They had survived the flood. She didn't need to know anything else.

She held out no hope at all of ever getting Anava back. Anava would become prey for the very first creatures that found her if she survived the flood at all.

Mora didn't let herself think about the baby. Mora had to keep these two children alive at all costs—and that meant feeding them.

She waited a long time before she pried their arms off. They kept crying while she held them at arm's length and assessed them for any injuries. They both had the same cuts, scratches, and bruises that she had. Other than that, both children seemed fine.

"We have to process this Gurlg for food," she told them. "I need you to help me. We're all alone out here, so we need to work hard and work together to survive. Can you do that? I need you both to step up and help the band. We're a band of three now. Okay? I need your help. Thena, I need you to start a fire right over there. Maeno, I want you to go around and collect any sticks you can find, but don't leave this clearing. Stay where you can see me and Thena. All right?"

The two children nodded while they wiped snot and tears off their faces. They were both still crying when they turned away to obey her.

She would probably wind up doing everything herself anyway, but she just had to keep going no matter what. Quitting wasn't an option.

She turned away to go butcher the Gurlg when the leaves rustled across the clearing. Zaedi stepped out into the open. He carried a miniature kukri that Hangman had made for him.

"Zaedi!" Mora rushed him and hugged him. "You're alive! I thought you were gone."

He looked back and forth between her and his younger siblings. "I thought you were all dead. I heard crying, so I came to see what it was." His eyes dipped to her chest. "Anava is gone, isn't she?"

"She got torn off me in the flood," Mora told him. "I don't know where she is."

He only nodded. "I thought so. Did you kill that Gurlg?"

"It was attacking Maeno and Thena. Come on, Zaedi. I need you to help me butcher it."

He went to work without complaint. He had grown up Godless. He knew exactly what to do and he didn't hesitate. His attitude got Thena and Maeno moving.

Mora and Zaedi started cutting up the Gurlg. She put a hunk of meat on the spit over the fire that Thena built with a bunch of Maeno's sticks. They all kept working while the meat cooked.

Mora left Zaedi to finish sectioning the Gurlg while she cut limbs from the jungle and built tripods to smoke as much of the meat as possible overnight. Zaedi didn't stop working when the other two sat down by the fire.

Mora cut up the fresh meat, served it to them, and kept back a portion for herself and Zaedi while she put another chunk on the fire.

"Do you know where we are, Mother?" Zaedi asked while they worked.

"I have no idea. I planned to follow the riverbed upstream as far as I could go. That's where Shadow's band will be—although they'll probably all be gone by the time we get there."

He bent over his work and mumbled under his breath. "Father isn't here. I'm the man of this family now."

"You're still uninitiated, but I'll be grateful for any help you can give me."

He fell into a thoughtful silence. This had been coming for him for a long time. He had been rushing to grow up and become an initiated man of the Godless Clan. He hated being a boy.

He kept working alongside her to cut the remaining meat into strips and hang them on the tripods. Maeno and Thena fell asleep by the fire long before Mora and Zaedi finished working.

"You should get some sleep, too, my son," she told him. "You'll be exhausted tomorrow."

"We need this food. We shouldn't go anywhere until we finish this, even if it means staying here for a few days."

She smiled at him and then looked away. "You'll be Kral of your band one day if you talk like that."

Now he was the one who looked away. "I could never be Kral the way Father is. I don't know how I could ever be as good as he is."

"You would grow a lot, learn to hunt and fight, and eventually marry and have a family of your own. You would grow in strength, initiate, and you would get to be a man any Godless would be proud to call their Kral. You wouldn't do it now. You might even get bigger than Hangman. He isn't the biggest man in the Clan."

"He's the best," Zaedi countered. "He doesn't have to be the biggest. He's the bravest, the smartest, and the most ruthless. That's what makes him Kral—not his size. Look at Viking and Legacy—and Alien. They were all proud to call him Kral.....and now he has to follow Shadow. It isn't right."

He grumbled these words with such bitter resentment that he took Mora aback. "You should be careful not to speak against your Kral like that. You might not agree with everything Shadow does. Shadow followed Butcher when Shadow and most of the men didn't agree with Butcher's way. No Kral can make decisions that everyone agrees with."

"Hangman does," Zaedi countered. "I never saw any of the men question his decisions. Everyone questions Shadow's decisions even if they don't say it out loud. I've seen them looking at each other behind his back."

She didn't know what to say. All the adults in the band could see the men questioning Shadow's leadership. The older children and uninitiated boys must have seen it, too.

Mora just didn't expect a seven-year-old boy to notice it. She shouldn't have been surprised. Zaedi had always been astute to the ways of men. He paid close attention to everything the men did. He was bound to notice that, too.

She decided to change the subject. "Do you remember Alien?"

"I remember him very well," Zaedi murmured. "He was an excellent man—and I remember Hammer. I wish I had been old enough to go with him."

Mora couldn't look at her son. "Hammer was an outstanding Kral and a great warrior. I'm sure his band is thriving out there somewhere."

"We should have gone with him," Zaedi mumbled. "We shouldn't have stayed with Shadow. We wouldn't be here now if we had gone with Hammer."

She didn't answer at all that time. She and Zaedi worked in silence for a while before she saw him rubbing his eyes. "Go to sleep, my son. We'll do as you say and stay here to process this meat. You don't have to hurry to get the work done."

"I want to. You're a woman. I should protect you and provide for you."

She laughed at him. "You're seven years old and I'm your mother. It's my job to protect and provide for you. Now go to sleep. You won't be any good to me tomorrow if you don't sleep now."

That convinced him. He went over to the fire, ate his share of the cooked meat, and curled up on the ground with his brother and sister.

Mora still had a lot of work to do to process the Gurlg. She had never had to process any creature this big—not by herself.

She worked for hours and cooked as much of the meat fresh as she thought she and the children could possibly eat before it all went bad. That cut down on the meat she had to cut to dry the strips out.

She had to stop and gather firewood to keep the fire going. She even started more than one fire and set up more than one tripod.

The children slept through it all. She exhausted herself long before sunrise, but she didn't let herself stop. She also didn't let herself think about Anava. Mora channeled all her care for her children into finishing this job.

These three children right here needed her. Wherever Anava was right now, she didn't need Mora.

Mora was still working by the time daylight crept over the jungle. The smell of blood and food brought the creatures out. She had to stop more than once when Abnormits discovered the dead Gurlg.

She finally gave it up. She had already carved off as much of the meat as she was likely to get.

The blood and the body would attract bigger, more dangerous creatures, so she dragged what was left of the carcass to a safe distance from camp.

She left the dead Gurlg near an Abnormit nest. She wanted the Abnormits to devour the remains before Demonex, Gorlocks, Krakelows, or any other large, dangerous creatures came near her camp.

She retreated to a safe distance, cut a stout club from one of the nearby trees, and hurled it into the nest's steep, conical mud walls.

Abnormits poured from inside, swarmed the area, and discovered the Gurlg carcass. They started eating it down to the bone and then devoured the bones until nothing remained.

Chapter 5

Hangman ran all night. He no longer felt the rain pelting his skin. He kept one hand on the cliff wall next to him and followed it around countless twists and turns to the end of the gorge. He didn't get there until daylight. Now he could see where he was.

The rain didn't stop even then. He climbed up to a high peak where he could see the whole landscape for miles around.

The cliffs dropped away from rugged mountains in steep valleys. He couldn't see their bottoms from here, but he did see the channel where Mora and the children had gotten swept away.

The Godless had camped on either side of the channel. He couldn't see individual people. He could only make out some dark spots on the sandy cliff walls.

The channel cut downward between the cliffs and vanished into another steep valley between the high mountains. Water kept pounding down the channel without stopping. It covered miles of territory before it plunged over the side of a steep waterfall.

He didn't let himself think that Mora and the children might not have survived. He would just keep searching until he found them. He didn't care if he succeeded or not. He just had to keep going.

He measured certain features of that valley rim so he would be able to recognize it. A sharp protruding point of rock stuck out of the cliff right next to where the waterfall fell over the edge. He hadn't seen a feature like that before.

Another cliff corner dropped away into a steep crevice. The crevice didn't plunge all the way to the valley floor. It just interrupted the cliff rim and made a mark there.

A high rock outcropping jutted into the air where that waterfall landed. Mora and the children would be down there. He could use these distinguishing features to identify these places even if he saw them from different angles.

He set off down the mountain, but he walked this time. The rain stopped during the morning. He worked his way closer to that one valley and climbed up on another outcropping to look over the side.

The waterfall ended in a massive pool at the bottom. A river flowed out of that pool. Whole trees churned in the flood. Debris, boulders, and dead creatures dotted the bank. He even saw dead Gorlocks and Crushers down there.

The thick, muddy torrent kept beating over and over itself as it rushed downstream. More and more water pounded down from above to fill the pool and spill into the riverbed.

He looked everywhere for a way to get down there, but he didn't see anything. He actually considered throwing himself over the waterfall and hoping for the best. At least he wouldn't have to worry about Mora and the children anymore.

He couldn't do that. They needed his help—wherever they were. He had to find them and rescue them from......well, from everything.

He wasn't paying enough attention to anything else around him. He barely noticed anything before a Boultar pelted out of the sky and collided with him full force.

It knocked him over and he tumbled off the outcropping. He wasn't close enough to the cliff edge to fall to his death. He fell between the outcropping and another pile of boulders right next to it.

He hit both sides of the cleft again and again until he fell down into a tight crack between the two rocks. He slammed down hard on a jagged floor and winced when the sharp points stabbed into his skin.

The Boultar tried again and again to get into the crack and grab him, but the rock protected him. He pried himself up into a sitting position and winced again when he saw the gashes and torn flesh cut by the rock.

He couldn't get out of here as long as the Boultar kept trying to get him. These mountains didn't have leaves to make any healing paste. He just had to live with the pain.

He did still have some of the cloth bandages he and Mora had collected over the years. He wrapped them around his wounds. His blood immediately soaked through them.

He wouldn't be able to do anything about it without leaf paste. He would only get that in the jungle and that meant getting down into the valley bottom.

The valley cut east to west across the riverbed at the base of that waterfall. The valley must have some head where he could get down into it. He just had to go there.

He couldn't waste any more time sitting around waiting for this stupid Boultar to go away. He crawled up the crack until he positioned himself right at the top where the two rocks came together.

The Boultar saw him, dove, and tried to wedge its feet into the crack. He grabbed the creature by its feet, yanked it down hard, and slammed the creature's body against the rock on both sides. The crack wasn't wide enough for the Boultar to fit through it.

The Boultar squawked and screeched, but not for long. Hangman held it with one hand and drove his kukri into its body with the other. He didn't like to let a creature this big go to waste, but he didn't have any firewood to cook it with.

He left the creature flopping and screeching in its death throes, climbed out of the crack, and took off running toward the head of the valley. He didn't get there until sunset, but his effort paid off. He found a path to the valley floor.

It was too dark to do anything now, so he climbed into the trees and went to sleep. He woke up and set off running again. He went into a trance where he no longer felt his hunger or his injuries. His own driving need to find Mora and the children pushed him to his limit.

He came to the base of the waterfall in the middle of the second day. He paced around it and looked up. He wouldn't have expected anything to survive that fall, but he refused to accept that Mora and the children were gone—not until he saw their bodies for himself.

He set off hiking downriver, but the sight of all these dead Gorlocks, Crushers, Demonex, and every other kind of creature—they brought him back to his senses. He could cook some of this food without having to hunt.

He built a quick fire, roasted a hunk of Gorlock meat, and kicked the fire out before he walked off downriver chewing the food. He didn't want to delay.

He had to stop again at sunset. He searched everywhere for any sign of human footprints to show that someone had walked away from the riverbank. He didn't find anything.

He did find a whole bunch of uprooted trees, massive stones torn out of their places and left strewn miles away from where they started, and whole swaths of countryside covered in mud and tangled vegetation ripped from the jungle.

He glanced around for somewhere to camp. That was the moment he spotted a bundle of hide lying twenty yards from the river. He recognized the strip of hide wrapped around it.

He walked over to it and stared down at the knot holding the bundle into a tube. He didn't have to turn the bundle over to know what he would find inside it.

He had been watching Mora tie that knot for seven years. No one tied knots like she did. Godless women used their own techniques for tying things.

He didn't turn the bundle over or look inside it. He stared at it for a long time and walked away to continue his journey.

He turned several bends in the riverbed before night fell and he couldn't go any further.

He climbed into the branches and found a place to spend the night. He fell asleep and woke up hours later in the small hours of the morning. Growling noises woke him up. He sat up and listened to Demonex prowling up and down the riverbank.

They fought over dead carcasses even though there were plenty here to go around. Hangman squatted on a thick branch and watched the creatures in the moonlight. They started out sharing the feast until fights broke out.

The noise brought Krakelows, Gorlocks, and Abnormits out of the jungle. They all crowded around, started eating the dead creatures, and then started to put the Demonex in danger.

The Krakelows and Abnormits pulled down two Demonex before the others got wise and backed off. They left the spoils to the Krakelows and Abnormits.

Hangman watched for a while and then drifted off again. He woke up in the morning and looked out at the riverbank. Most of the same creatures were still out there gorging themselves, fighting each other, and even killing each other.

They only succeeded in providing more food for the creatures left behind. Hangman would have liked to follow the riverbank, but he didn't dare to go out there with this going on.

He traveled through the branches for a long way. He could see the river from here. He even saw some dead men out there. He didn't see any dead women or children.

He didn't recognize which Clan the dead men belonged to. They wore a strange combination of clothing and he couldn't get close enough to examine them.

He kept going, and in another few hours, he left the part of the river with all the dead creatures around it.

He descended to the ground and followed the river some more, but he had to climb back into the trees pretty soon when more creatures came to the river for some reason. They might have been hunting or they might have come for some other reason.

He stayed in the branches after that, slept another night, and eventually arrived at the edge of the trees. The river stretched through a broad open plane from here.

The river led to another giant waterfall plunging into another vertical gorge. He couldn't see the bottom nor could he see any way into it from here.

The sun was already going down by the time he made it to the head of the falls. He had to backtrack and spend the night in the trees for safety.

He returned to the waterfall the next day, but he only looked over the side for a few seconds. Mora and the children were down there. He didn't know how he knew this, but he had never been more certain of anything in his life.

He might have already slipped over the edge into madness. He might have lost his mind in grief and convinced himself that Mora and the children were still alive when there was absolutely no way they could have survived that flood.

He didn't care if he had gone completely insane or not. He had to keep going no matter what. Stopping meant admitting to himself that they really were gone. He wasn't ready to do that yet. He probably never would be ready to admit that.

He took off at a run around the edge of the valley. He had to stop more than once just to spend the night and get some sleep. It took him days to run around the valley rim until he found his way back to the same waterfall.

He searched every corner of the valley rim. He didn't find any way to get down there. Mora and the children were trapped down there and he was trapped on the outside with no way to rejoin them.

Chapter 6

M ora gathered up some big handfuls of dried meat and packed them into a smaller shoulder bag for Zaedi. "You carry this food, my son."

"Yes, Mother," he replied. He had been helping her for three days to dry as much of the Gurlg meat as possible. He had also helped her locate some dead creatures along the riverbank.

Mora and Zaedi had skinned the creatures and stitched the hides into bags for all three children. They did this task while they waited for the meat to dry enough for traveling fare.

Mora loaded the dried meat into all the children's bags. She packed her own bags to bursting. She didn't even know how long the family would be able to travel on this food before she had to hunt again.

Zaedi carried his two much smaller kukris tucked into his waistband. They were hardly longer than Mora's forearm, but he was learning how to use them.

She got the children moving upriver. The family returned to the riverbank. "Keep your eyes open for dead people," she told her children.

"Why do we care about dead people?" Zaedi asked. "They can't threaten us."

She laughed at him. "I was thinking we could take their weapons to arm Thena and Maeno."

Zaedi made a face at his younger siblings. "They can't do anything."

"They might be able to do something. Anyway, neither of them will be able to do as much unarmed as they will be able to do something armed—so look around for some weapons."

The party kept walking all day. She stopped the children whenever they complained about being tired.

"At least we can stop now," Zaedi mumbled. "Shadow never stopped."

"How much do you remember about the journey south from the northern valley?"

He nodded. "I remember that. Hangman was much nicer about stopping. He never would have left anyone behind."

Mora didn't answer. She should have corrected Zaedi for criticizing his Kral—except that Zaedi had never accepted Shadow as his Kral. Zaedi had only been four years old when Hangman's band met up with and joined Shadow's band.

She found it hard to believe that Zaedi had been aware enough even then to recognize his father's value as Kral. Hangman's men admired him and followed his orders to the letter. They all followed him without question.

Even Hammer and his men had always followed Hangman's lead. The women and children in Hangman's band had always obeyed his decisions even when the people didn't like it. Why?

Mora didn't have to wonder. He asked his people or at least explained to them why he wanted to do something. He never demanded that they just accept his word because he was Kral.

She could count a dozen incidents when he told his people straight out why they had to leave some protected place and move when they were all tired and aching from the journey.

Zaedi was too smart not to notice the palpable air of tension in Shadow's band. The hostility radiating between Shadow and the rest of his men poisoned the atmosphere.

That atmosphere was so astronomically different from the cohesion of Hangman's band. All his people and all his men had been bound by mutual respect and shared hardship for years. Their cohesion never broke—not once.

Hangman had bent over backward to make sure it never broke. He had given Hammer and Red all the autonomy they could possibly ask for. Hangman never asked for blind obedience and he would never, ever demand it. That wasn't his way.

Mora got lost in her own thoughts—mostly about her husband. She really did get lucky when she married him. Now she was alone with these children.

She would have to rely on all her skill if she had a prayer of surviving and keeping her children alive. She couldn't risk injuring or killing herself.

She found some dead men by the river a few hours later. She didn't recognize what Clan they came from. Their clothes and hairstyles didn't match anything she'd seen or even read about.

They carried weapons—metal weapons. She retrieved three different knives and some longer blades. These weren't as long as her two Renegade blades and they were too big for Maeno and Thena.

She gave them a knife each. "Now listen to me very carefully, my loves," she told them. "Every creature in this jungle is out to eat you—and all of us. I know you're very young, but you're Godless nonetheless. It's time for you to step up and learn how to defend yourselves. If anything attacks us, you'll draw your weapon and fight back. Is that clear? You can't go your whole lives expecting Zaedi and me to defend you. The sooner you start learning, the better."

Thena said, "Yes, Mother. We will."

Maeno stared down at the knife in his hand. He didn't have a clue what to do with it.

She took it from him and tucked it into the waistband of his loin-cloth. He forgot all about it as soon as she did that. He would just have to grow into his strength as a fully initiated warrior when the time came.

She couldn't imagine him ever getting big enough to initiate, but it would happen before she knew it. She had to get him there in one piece.

She was definitely starting to see Zaedi old enough to initiate. She could picture him as a much bigger, stronger version of the boy he was now. He would be ready to initiate.

He resembled his father in their attitude. Zaedi questioned everything. He didn't like doing things another person's way. He had his own ideas about how the band ought to run.

He gave his brother and sister hard looks even though he was barely old enough to defend himself. He wouldn't be able to defend himself against anything as big as a Demonex, much less something bigger like a Gorlock or a Krakelow.

Mora probably wouldn't be able to defend any of them against that, either. She would have to come up with some other way to deal with all of this—like hiding herself and her children from danger if it came to that.

They set off up the river again, but she retreated into the jungle when night fell. All three children could climb well, so the canopy would be the best place for them to sleep.

She wove vines and branches together make a nest for Maeno and Thena to sleep in. Zaedi stayed up with her and they both listened to the jungle sounds until he fell asleep, too. She stayed up much later.

She wouldn't be able to take these small children through the gorge country—not the way the Godless band did. The band barely survived with two dozen fully grown fighting men on hand to protect everyone.

The men couldn't save everyone from creature attacks from the air. The three children would draw Ridgebeaks and Boultars by the dozen. She wouldn't be able to fight them by herself. She had to come up with some other solution.

She would have stayed up all night thinking about it, but her care for her children forced her to go to sleep. She had to be alert and functioning tomorrow morning and every morning after this.

She was the last line of defense. Everything she knew and had learned from the Godless—she had to use all of it to protect her children even if it meant breaking the rules.

What was she even thinking? There were no rules. She couldn't afford to do things the Godless way—not if it put her children in danger.

Any threat to her would put her children in danger. She had to stay alive. She had to stay healthy. She had to stay rested, alert, functioning, and uninjured.

She kept her children in the branches the next day. The family couldn't travel as fast this way, but she had no reason to go back to the riverbank.

She could see it perfectly well from here. Dangerous creatures prowled out there for dead bodies and anything else they could find.

She traveled upriver and parallel to the water's edge kept for the whole day. The children's presence attracted the creatures' attention.

A mob of Demonex spotted the family and climbed up into the trees to intercept Mora and her children.

Mora retreated into the higher canopy where the branches wouldn't support the Demonex's weight.

The highest canopy left the family exposed to Boultar attacks from the air, but Mora kept her children there for hours until the sun went down and the Demonex finally left.

"How far do we have to travel, Mother?" Thena asked.

"As far as it takes," Zaedi told her.

"Why do we have to travel at all?" Maeno complained. "I don't want to travel. Why can't we stay here?"

"We can't stay here alone. It's too dangerous," Zaedi told them. "We have to at least try to rejoin the band. Don't you at least want to see Father?"

"He could come here and stay with us," Maeno suggested.

"You don't know what you're talking about," Zaedi fired back. "He doesn't even know where we are and he wouldn't be able to protect us by himself even if he did. He isn't here. We're by ourselves and we can't protect ourselves. We need the band for that. That's why people live in bands. Don't you at least know that much?"

Thena turned to Mora. "How do we rejoin the band, Mother?"

"I'm not sure, my love. I don't know where we would rejoin the band or which direction they were traveling. I only know that we'll never rejoin them if we stay here. That's why we're traveling."

"These mountains seem to come together over there near the head of the river," Zaedi pointed out. "We got into this riverbed somehow. There must be a way to get out and climb back to where we came from."

"Let's hope so," Mora replied. "Now it's time for all of you to go to sleep. Tomorrow is another long day."

She bedded down the children in another woven nest. This time, she climbed into it with them and went straight to sleep. All this thinking accomplished nothing, but she would have to make a decision pretty soon.

She shouldn't take her children out into the gorge country if it would be too dangerous for them to survive. Staying here alone would be better as long as the family stood a better chance of surviving here.

The next day passed uneventfully except that Mora had to direct her children to avoid certain creatures. The family had to climb higher to avoid creatures coming at them from the ground and descend to avoid creatures coming from the treetops.

The surrounding cliffs loomed higher as the family got closer to the head of the valley. A giant waterfall pounded down from cliffs a thousand feet high—or they looked that way.

The waterfall fed into the river a dozen miles upstream. Mora came within sight of the waterfall and stopped her children in the canopy.

The waterfall's constant boom drowned out all other noise. Mora stopped where she was, sat down on a branch, and stared up at the falls. She didn't have to take her children all the way there. She could see the situation well enough from here.

"Why are we stopping?" Zaedi asked.

"Look," Mora told him. "You can see the falls and the cliffs. We wouldn't be able to get out that way."

"But....we have to," he pointed out. "We have to get out some way."

Mora turned around and surveyed the countryside through which she and her children had been traveling. These steep cliffs surrounded a massive valley. She had been seeing these cliffs all the way here.

"There is no other way out of this valley," she told him. "There might be a way out to the south, but it would take us days to travel all that way. Even if we found a way out, we would have to travel through the gorge country with no food, no trees, and no protection." She sighed and turned back in the direction from which she had just come. "Let's go."

"Where are we going?" Thena asked.

"We're going back to the rocks where I found you. We have to make a long camp where we'll be protected and where we can stay for a long time."

"You mean.....we have to stay alone?" Zaedi asked.

She shrugged. "I'm open to suggestions if you have any, my son. Think about it. We'll make a long camp where we can stay while we explore this valley. That's the best way we'll find a way out if there is any way out. You let me know if you come up with a better plan than that."

He furrowed his brow in deep thought. She found herself hoping he *would* come up with a solution—something she hadn't thought of.

None of her children would be satisfied to stay here forever—and neither would she. They would have to find a way out of this valley—which meant making a much more detailed search of the terrain. They could only do that from a place of safety.

The trip back to the rocks took a lot longer than the trip here. The creatures along this route knew about the family now. All four had to work together to repel constant attacks and deal with injuries.

Mora kept her children in the branches the whole way there. None of them set foot on the ground except when Mora went alone to go get water from the river each day.

Chapter 7

Z aedi withdrew into himself on the journey back to the rocks. He became hard and coldly determined. Whatever part of him had still been a soft, innocent boy—it died on that trip.

He glared out at the surrounding jungle through narrowed eyes and studied everything much more closely than before.

He seemed to take it extremely seriously that he was the only person here who would ever become a Godless warrior. He had been busting to become one all his young life.

Now he saw himself becoming one long before his time. He seemed to recognize that he was still too small to be a true warrior. He could barely fight a Gurlg chick, but he took the defense of his mother, sister, and younger brother much more seriously.

Zaedi assigned himself to stand guard when Mora worked on any detail of the family's traveling needs. Zaedi stood guard over her pretty much all the time. He only slackened his vigilance when he went to sleep.

She didn't correct him or try to change his attitude. She didn't encourage him to slacken his vigilance or to stay a boy as long as he could. She was too grateful for his help. She needed all the help he could give her.

The trip took them another five days to return to the rocks. The family searched the area until Mora found a stand of rock where she could make her camp. A bunch of outcroppings stood near enough to each other to form walls around a clearing in the center.

The jungle grew thick overhead to protect the spot from aerial attacks. Undergrowth covered most of the rocks to hide the clearing.

A few different openings entered the clearing between the outcroppings. She directed her children to gather as many fallen branches from the surrounding jungle as they could drag. Maeno and Thena worked together.

Mora cut the branches, stood them on their ends in the gaps, and wove them together to make walls. She wrapped the woven vines around the surrounding rocks and blocked every entrance but one. That was the only way into or out of the clearing.

She built another wall for the entrance, but she didn't lash the wall into place. She positioned it so she could remove and replace it when she needed to.

Now a creature could only get in by climbing up the outcropping or dropping from the canopy directly overhead. It wasn't a perfect arrangement, but it was better than nothing.

The outcroppings had different hollows around their bases in different parts of each outcropping. These hollows acted as rooms where the children could crawl in and hide from the air.

The family relaxed in their new camp, now that the children knew they didn't have to travel anymore. Mora spent the rest of the day building a shelter against one of the rocks. She constructed it over the hollows to take advantage of their protection.

Zaedi stood in the center of the camp and cast a flinty look around. "I don't like staying in the shelter. I want to be out here where I can see and hear everything."

"You can stay out here if you want to," Mora told him. "You're old enough to come and go as you please. You can sleep in that hollow over there. Then you'll be able to see and hear if anything comes into our camp without us knowing about it."

He nodded. "I'll do that. Good thinking, Mother."

She smiled at him. She would have liked to hug him or stroke his hair, but she sensed him moving too far away from her for that. He was already starting to distance himself from the world of women.

She didn't like the idea of raising him in isolation from other Godless men. She would just have to hope he remembered enough from people like his father, Alien, Hammer, and the others. Zaedi would know how to grow into a man like them.

He wouldn't be able to initiate himself, though. Only other Godless men could do that.

She would come up against the same problem when Zaedi got old enough. The family would have to leave this valley—and both Zaedi and Thena would have to go to the gathering.

Mora didn't want to stay in this valley alone. Her mission would be to search the surrounding cliffs and find a way out.

She and her children sat on the ground, shared their food and water, and talked until it got dark. Zaedi slept in his hollow across the camp while Mora took the younger two children into the shelter.

"I want to stay outside with Zaedi," Maeno announced.

"You're too young to stay out there," she told him. "Wait a little while until you get bigger."

Now Maeno was the one who scowled. He was only three, but he could get very stubborn and determined when he wanted something.

Mora would have her hands full with these two boys. She would have to direct their energy toward useful purposes—like hunting and protecting their sister.

She took all three children with her when she left their long camp the next morning. She didn't trust leaving any of them alone even.

She traveled a mile out into the jungle away from the river and got them to help her dig a deep pit in another clearing. Then she cut strong limbs from the surrounding jungle.

"What are we doing here, Mother?" Zaedi asked.

"I'm building a pit trap to snare animals for food." She hacked the ends of the limbs to carve them to points. "It works better if we could use some kind of bait, but this will be better than nothing."

He furrowed his brow. "That isn't the Godless way. We should hunt."

"We would take our lives in our hands every time we hunted. I would take my life in my hands every time I hunted. Something might happen to me and you three children would be left alone. I can't risk that."

She built herself a ladder and climbed down into the pit. It came up to the height of her head. All three children worked together to lower the sharpened spikes down to her. She anchored them in the bottom of the pit before she climbed out.

"Now we need to weave mats to cover the pit and conceal it."

The children worked willingly. Mora laid thinner branches over the pit, covered them with the mats, and scattered leaves and debris over the mats to hide the trap.

These traps might not work without a warthog or something to lure the prey here. No creature might fall into the traps.

She occupied the children by building another five pit traps around the area. The family was already starting to run low on food by the time they finished the last trap.

She taught the children to go around and check all the traps each day in case a creature fell into them. She didn't hold out much hope that it would work, but on the fifth day, they discovered a dead Gorlock impaled on the spikes in one of the traps.

The family spent the next four days processing all the Gorlock meat and drying it for long-term storage. Mora and Zaedi butchered and skinned the Gorlock inside the trap and carried the hide and giant haunches of the meat back to the long camp.

Mora hacked up what was left, reformed the trap, and left all the offal, bones, and leftover scraps around the trap to lure other creatures that might want to scavenge on the remains.

She took her children back to their long camp and they started cutting up the meat to dry it for storage. The process made Zaedi thoughtful. He walked around wearing a permanent frown of deep thought.

"You came from the Followers," he finally blurted out while they hung the meat on tripods to dry.

"You know I did, my son," Mora replied over her shoulder.

"And you're using their methods now, aren't you? These traps and things—you used them in the Followers."

"All the time," she told him. "The Followers don't hunt. We don't risk human life to hunt anything."

"Do you regret becoming Godless?" he asked.

"Not at all. I'm proud to be Godless. I'm only doing this because I'm the only adult around to take care of you children. All three of you will die if something happens to me—and it wouldn't be safe for me to take you hunting. I'm doing it this way because I have to. I wouldn't do it at all if we were with the band."

He fell silent for a minute. "What else do the Followers do?"

"We don't fight other Clans—or dangerous creatures. The Followers believe in protecting human life at all costs. Fighting means people can get hurt and killed. We hide or avoid creatures and enemies."

"You've been doing that on this trip, haven't you? You've been doing it that way since we wound up here."

She finally turned around and faced him. "It would make no sense for me to fight something I know I can't defeat. What possible advantage could I gain from fighting this Gorlock instead of killing it with a trap? You're thinking like a Godless warrior, my son, and that's the way it should be, but I'm not a Godless warrior. I'm a woman, I'm alone, and I'm responsible for keeping all three of you children alive. We could be stuck in this valley for years. I can't follow the Godless way. I couldn't follow the Godless way even if I wanted to. That would be the quickest way to get us all killed."

Chapter 8

Z aedi fell into another deep silence after his conversation with Mora the Followers. Zaedi didn't speak again while he and Mora worked. He didn't break the silence until they finished work and sat down to eat at last.

"Tell me more about what the Followers do," he blurted out.

"Well, for a start, we gather as much knowledge as we can from the ancients and we pass it down to our children. That's why we take such care to keep people alive as long as possible. The grandparents and great-grandparents have learned a lot in their lives. We would lose their knowledge if we let anything happen to them. They're too valuable when it comes to passing down that information to the next generation. We work to build that knowledge and add to what the grandparents and great-grandparents already know."

He frowned at her. "How do you gather information about the ancients when they aren't around anymore?"

"We go into their cities and study their books and texts left behind. We read how they did things and we study their tools and possessions."

"What does, 'read' mean?"

Mora sighed and used her forefinger to draw the letters of the alphabet in the dirt at her feet.

"These symbols represent sounds that form words. This word right here means, 'to hunt'. Every word in our language can be written out like this. The ancients used this system to record how they did things, what they were thinking about, how they interacted with each other—everything about their society. You've heard the stories about the Renegades using ancient weapons against us and your father and I blowing up their ammunition store. I only did that because I knew about it from reading ancient texts and learning how they did things. The Renegades found out how to use those weapons by capturing and interrogating Followers. The Follower Clan is the only Clan that knows about the ancients. We learn about ancient times by reading their texts and passing that information down from one generation to another."

Zaedi went into another long silence before he asked, "Does my father know how to read?"

Mora snorted. "Are you joking? He would never do anything as Follower as that. He hates the Followers."

"But he doesn't *always* do things the Godless way, either, does he? He doesn't always confront his enemies head-on the way the Godless are supposed to. He spends more time ambushing them, springing surprise attacks on them, and hitting them in ways they don't expect. He doesn't always give them the warning he should give them—and he doesn't make the uninitiated boys stay away from the other men. He doesn't always follow the letter of the law."

Mora had to take a minute to decide how to answer. She never expected to have a conversation like this with a seven-year-old.

Zaedi was definitely growing up fast. He probably wouldn't have said this much if they had been anywhere else or around anyone else. All of this might be coming together in his head for the first time now because he found himself isolated with only her for company.

"Your father adapted his methods to the situation in which he found himself—kind of like we are now," she explained. "He had to do things differently because he didn't have enough fighting men to attack his enemies head on. He had to withdraw at times to save his band. He had to avoid his enemies at times when he knew he couldn't win. Attacking would have gotten the whole band wiped out—and he had no choice but to rely on Hammer and the other uninitiated boys. None of us would have survived if Hangman had strictly followed the Godless way. That would have been foolhardy. He wouldn't have been doing his job as Kral if he did that."

"Then are you saying Shadow didn't do his job as Kral by accepting Hammer's band and letting the men marry those girls?"

Mora checked herself a second time before she answered. "I'm not saying Shadow did or didn't do his job as Kral. I'm saying Hangman wouldn't have done it that way. Think about it. Hangman could have gotten defensive and resisted Hammer becoming Kral of his own band. Hangman could have tried to force Hammer to become subordinate, but Hangman didn't do that. Hangman was the one who told Hammer and all the rest of us that Hammer was Kral of his own band. Hangman made an alliance with Hammer as an equal to protect both bands. Hangman promised the girls to Hammer and his men to keep the peace between the two bands. Hangman had every reason to stay on good terms with Hammer. Hangman went to extraordinary lengths to make sure Hammer and his men got exactly what they wanted from the alliance—and it worked. Hammer and his men stayed with us and protected us. We wouldn't have made it back to Shadow's band without Hammer's help."

"Then what are you saying Shadow did?"

Mora raised her hands. "I don't think Shadow fully appreciated the situation for what it was until after it was too late. He didn't understand what all of us had been going through while we were away. He didn't understand why Hangman had to do things differently."

Zaedi only hesitated a split second. "I want you to teach me to read."

Mora's head shot up. "You do?"

He nodded. "Could you do it? Do you remember how?"

"Of course, but......That isn't the Godless way."

"Neither is using traps and snares to catch food. If you're right, then this information could benefit our Clan."

"How would it benefit us *here*?"

"I don't know. Maybe it would benefit me another time after I rejoined the band."

Mora studied her son. She didn't expect this from him. She expected him to go to the farthest extreme to make himself one-thousand-percent Godless no matter what. She wouldn't have been surprised if he refused to eat meat that came from a pit trap.

She had to think about it for a long time. All the Godless had been seeing her use her knowledge to benefit the Clan. None of the others ever asked her to teach them before.

"You said yourself it benefits the Clan to pass down the information from generation to generation," he went on. "All that knowledge will die with you if you don't teach someone. We're alone here with no one around. No one will come down on you for doing things the Follower way." He stared back at her through narrowed eyes. "Why do you hesitate? Do you think I can't learn? Do you think I'm not smart enough?"

"No, it isn't that. I'm certain you are smart enough. We teach children as young as Maeno how to read. It isn't that difficult once you learn how."

"Then why don't you agree?"

"I just.....I don't know. I've dedicated myself to being Godless all these years. It's hard for me to switch back into that way of thinking ....." She shrugged it off. "I guess I already am, so I have no reason not to. All right. Come over here and we'll get started."

He got up immediately and crossed the camp to sit next to her. She considered erasing the writing she'd already made in the dirt. Then she changed her mind.

She pointed to the first letters of the alphabet that she'd already written out. "See these symbols? Each one represents a sound. This one says, 'ahh'. These sounds are what make up the words we use to talk about things. This one says, 'buh' as in the word, 'Boultar'. So if you were going to write out the word, 'Boultar', you would start with this letter."

"What's a letter?" Thena asked.

"'Letter' is the word we use for each of these symbols. This one can make a 'kuh' sound or a 'ssss' sound depending on where it's used and how it's used."

Maeno came over and crawled into Mora's lap to listen and watch what she was doing. Thena sat down next to Zaedi and studied the letters intently.

"This down here is the word, 'hunt' like I told you," Mora went on. "The first letter says, 'hhh', the second letter says, 'uh', the third letter says, 'nnn' and the last letter says, 'tuh'. See what I mean?"

Zaedi nodded in silence.

Mora went on with the lesson. She'd gone through this speech more times than she could count starting when she was Zaedi's age teaching children as young as Maeno.

Teaching these children to read without any written material would be difficult but not impossible.

The project gave her a thrill unlike any she could remember. Zaedi was right. Passing this information down to the next generation wasn't just a good idea. It was critical to the Clan's survival.

He would need as much information as he could get if he ever became Kral of his band. He would be an asset to any Kral if he had this information and knew where to get more of it.

Chapter 9

Hangman sat in the crook of some jungle branches and braided a rope out of vines. He only used one strand of vines for each piece of the braid, so the rope only turned out as thick as his thumb. He didn't care about that.

He'd camped in this jungle for almost a week near the top of the valley where he surmised that Mora and the children must have gone over the falls. He had to get down there some way or other.

He had searched the valley rim three times and still not found any way in. So he had to come up with another plan. There was only one way in and that was to go over the side.

He had been hunting for himself and going through all the usual camp chores to keep himself alive while he braided a rope long enough to make it as far as the valley floor.

He had been working on this rope tirelessly in all his free time. He still had not made the rope long enough to touch the bottom.

The last thing in the world that he wanted was to climb down and come to the end of the rope still hundreds of feet off the ground. He would rather not climb down at all than end up in a disastrous situation like that.

He worked on the rope for three hours before he used up all the vines he'd collected. He coiled up the rope he'd already made and climbed down to the ground.

He had to drape the rope crossways across his torso so he could carry it all. It was a long, long rope—the longest he'd ever made.

He kept an eye on the countryside on his way to the cliff edge. All the dead carcasses washed up in the flood had made the surviving creatures much bolder, especially this close to the river.

The water had died back after the rain stopped. The river left even more debris, uprooted trees, and bodies of every species, including people. None of them were Godless and none of them were Mora or the children.

He stopped at the cliff edge, tied a large rock to the end of the rope, and lowered it over the side. He had been doing this for so long that he had perfected a method for detecting the bottom of the valley floor.

He had marked off on his rope how far he had extended it last time. He didn't have to check until he came to that mark. Then he lowered the rope a little farther and bounced the rock up and down to see if it bumped into anything solid.

He had crawled up to the very edge of the cliff on his belly to make sure there was nothing at the bottom to interfere with this project. He wouldn't have hit anything that wasn't close enough to the ground for him to survive a fall from that height.

He lowered the rope all the way to its end and finally bumped the rock against something. He raised and lowered it more than once. It thumped with a soft kind of thud like it was touching the ground.

He checked it for five minutes before he proceeded with the next phase of his experiment. He lashed the rope around another much larger rock at the edge of the cliff and flattened himself to the bare stone.

He pushed himself forward and looked over the side. The rock hung from the rope four feet off the ground. He had to use the extra length to tie off the rope. It worked. Now he had a rope the right length.

This rope wasn't thick enough for him to climb down. He planned to use this rope as one of five strands the same length and braid them together to make a much thicker, stronger rope the same length.

He wouldn't have to keep coming back to test it—not until he got a rope he thought could support his weight.

He pushed himself back from the edge and stood up to untie the rope. He could take all the time in the world to braid his rope. He would get down into that valley one way or the other. He would find out if Mora and the children were there.

He wouldn't decide what to do after that until he satisfied himself that they *weren't* there. They might have all died in the flood. He admitted that to himself.

If they did go over these falls and they did survive, then they were trapped in this valley with no way out. They would need his help more than ever down there.

He bent over to untie the rope—and a deep thump vibrated through the ground. More followed. He knew that sound. He looked up in time to see five massive Crushers stomping out of the jungle.

They followed the river and surveyed the surrounding terrain searching for more dead carcasses to scavenge. The Crushers saw him standing out in the open totally unprotected.

He straightened up and his hands migrated to his kukris, but he wouldn't be able to fight this many Crushers. He couldn't even back up to get away from them—not without falling over the cliff to his death.

He glanced right and left as the creatures moved in. Running away would leave him just as exposed. He would have to run past them to get to the jungle. He probably wouldn't even be able to outrun them.

He hesitated just a split second too long—long enough for them to spread out and surround him. They saw him trapped. There was no way out—and then he realized. He did have a way out.

He took his hands off his kukris, picked up the rope, and threw three more loops around the rock. He took that instant to twist the strand over itself four times. He had pulled this trick before on the Renegades. It would work even better on the Crushers. They weren't the smartest creatures in the jungle.

He braced himself for the assault. The Crushers picked up speed to charge him. He counted down the seconds as they closed around him—and lunged.

Three of the five rushed in first with the other two right behind them. He jumped clear at the last possible second and flung himself over the side of the cliff.

The Crushers' own momentum sent the first three wheeling out into space. Their enraged roars dwindled and they fell away into the vast silence.

The fourth Crusher skidded and tried to correct, but not soon enough. One of its feet crashed over the side right on top of Hangman's head.

The creature's foot sent a few broken hunks of rock smashing down into his skull and shoulders, but he held onto that rope for all he was worth.

The Crusher floundered and tried to claw its way back onto solid ground, but its own efforts knocked it off balance. The creature somersaulted over the edge and came perilously close to colliding with Hangman.

He ducked and huddled against the cliff while the enormous creature pitched head over heel past him into the void.

The last Crusher stopped in time and peered over the side. It looked out across the valley probably trying to figure out what had happened to its friends. They weren't here anymore. The Crusher was all alone.

The creature didn't look down to see Hangman dangling there by his fingernails. He held his breath and plastered himself to the cliff face praying to High Heaven that the creature didn't see him.

The Crusher eventually grunted under its breath and stomped away. Hangman hung there shaking like a leaf for a long time before he summoned the nerve to pull himself up. He didn't dare to look down at the vast chasm beneath his feet.

He finally dragged himself over the edge and flopped there gasping and trembling. That was a close one. He couldn't let anything like that happen again.

He took a long time to sit up. He only did it when he saw Boultars in the sky. They would come for him the longer he stayed out here in the open.

He untied his rope. At least he knew now that he needed at least four strands to support his weight on the trip down. He would probably need more than that. The strain would increase the lower he got to the ground.

He took the rope back to his campsite in the canopy and took some time to calm down and get something to eat. He wouldn't leave the jungle again until he was ready to test his new, much thicker rope.

He spent the rest of the day gathering vines and braiding more rope. He could work much more quickly now. He had enough food. He didn't have to leave his campsite except to gather more vines. He didn't have to keep checking the length.

He didn't stop braiding until the sun went down and it got too dark to see. He woke up at first light the next morning and spent every waking hour braiding his rope and then braiding six strands together.

That should be strong enough. He checked the length, lugged the rope to the side of the cliff, tied it around the very base of the rock to secure it, and threw the rope over the edge.

He had made this rope with footholds at strategic intervals so he didn't have to lower himself by arm strength alone.

He also wanted to be able to climb out when the time came. He wouldn't want to pull himself all the way up. He probably couldn't have done that even if he tried.

He took a few deep breaths, crawled to the edge, and inched his legs over. He had to cling to the rope and feel around with his feet before he found one of the footholds. He stepped into it and put his weight on it before he climbed the rest of the way over.

He didn't look down except to place his feet in the loops one after another. The climb down to the ground took a lot longer than he expected.

He stopped at the bottom and looked up. He would be screwed if anyone came along and found this rope. He wouldn't be able to get out of this valley any other way.

He turned around and faced the countryside at the base of the valley. It was perfectly flat as far as the eye could see with the same sheer cliffs surrounding the valley in all directions.

It was a big valley comprising almost fifty square miles of terrain completely blocked in by cliffs. Now he had to search the whole thing to find out if Mora and the children were here.

Chapter 10

Mora and her children strode down the riverbank heading south. They had searched the valley in ever-widening circles and still not come to the outer cliff walls.

The four of them would take weeks longer or maybe even months before they found a way out of here—if there was a way out. Mora would have to see if the way out led to more gorge country. She would have to decide if she could risk such a journey.

She had been thinking about this a lot in the weeks since she and her children had been stranded here.

She might have to wait another five years or maybe longer for her children to get older. Then maybe they would be able to make the journey without getting killed.

Zaedi had become more ferociously ruthless with every passing day. He never hesitated to draw his weapons whenever he felt the need.

Thena had stepped up, too. She and Zaedi went out on short hunting trips near their long camp. They practiced killing anything they could find that was small enough for them to tackle together.

They brought food back to the camp all the time. They provided a good portion of the family's needs to supplement anything Mora caught in her pit traps.

Maeno still hadn't gotten the message about defending himself. He still lived in a fantasy world of sticks, rocks, leaves, and brightly colored stones. He hadn't drawn his weapon even once since the family came to live here.

Mora had scavenged a bunch of weapons from dead people along the river. She didn't search there much anymore, but the open ground was the quickest way to cover the miles to search farther afield to find out more about the valley.

Entire populations of Gorlocks, Crushers, Demonex, Gurlgs, and Stalkions lived in this valley. Ridgebeaks nested in the cliffs and Boultars swooped over the valley from the surrounding mountains.

The jungle here had all the same Bliztwords and Cursed Sand. Dushags lived in the river. They came out more often, now that the floodwaters had died down and left the water clearer.

Ashtaws didn't live in the valley. She had no idea why. They were the only familiar creature she knew that didn't live here.

Mora didn't see how the creatures got into the valley in the first place, but enough of them lived here and reproduced themselves to keep the family fed for a long time—as long as Mora chose to stay here.

She checked the jungle on her left to make sure no creatures came out of the trees from that direction to ambush her and her children in the open. Zaedi startled her back to her senses by stopping in his tracks.

"Mother," he growled. "We should get back to the trees."

She turned around and saw what he was looking at. Another pack of Demonex loped out of the jungle on the right side of the river—the opposite side from the family.

"Let's go." She grabbed Maeno by the hand. "Get to the trees! Run!"

Zaedi and Thena took off at a dead sprint. Mora had to keep slowing down to stay with Maeno. He didn't recognize the danger quickly enough.

She ended up scooping him into her arms and charging away just as the Demonex made it to the water's edge. They leapt across and burst into a run to bring the family down.

Zaedi and Thena vaulted into the branches and vanished into the high canopy. Mora had to stop at the edge of the trees and boost Maeno into the branches. "Climb!" She cast a desperate glance behind her. "Climb as high as you can!"

The Demonex made it halfway across the open ground before Maeno lifted his weight out of her arms. She could finally clamber up there and join him. They barely made it to a safe distance before the Demonex entered the jungle and sprang into the branches, too.

All four of the family had to climb all the way up to the smallest branches to escape. "It doesn't look like we'll be doing any exploring today," Thena remarked.

"We'll just have to keep trying," Mora told them. "We'll go check our traps. We'll have plenty to do if we caught anything."

Zaedi squinted southward. "I wish I was older. I would go alone the way Father did."

Mora didn't answer. She often wished she could explore the valley alone without taking her children with her—or that they were old enough to do it for her.

Zaedi's need to leave this valley would only get stronger as he grew older. He would become determined to find older men to initiate him.

She found it harder and harder to think of him as a child even though he was just a little boy. He no longer acted like a boy at all. Thena didn't act like a six-year-old girl. She seemed to be in a rush to grow up, too.

Both of them had become so much harder and more serious just in the last couple of weeks. They scared Mora, but she couldn't bring herself to regret it. A situation like this was bound to sober anyone. It certainly sobered her.

They had to wait for hours before the Demonex finally gave up and left. Mora and her two older children spent the time working on their reading. They couldn't write on the ground, so they just talked.

Mora asked each of them to spell certain words from memory and then she asked them to spell out whole sentences. They had inhaled everything she taught them. They could read complex sentences she wrote out for them on the ground.

She had developed a similar pattern to the pencils the Followers used to teach children to write. She charred sticks in the fire and had Zaedi and Thena write on pieces of stone she collected from the outcroppings near their long camp.

She posed them challenges to write stories in short paragraphs. Then she had them swap their stones and read each other's work out loud.

Maeno drank in every detail of their conversation. He had already learned the alphabet. He was starting to read simple words like, 'mat', 'cat', and 'at'.

Zaedi and Thena liked to quiz each other on their spelling words. Each of them tried to pose the other some word to stump each other with something they couldn't spell.

They entertained Mora for hours with this game. Each of them would ask her for a word they didn't know or they would pick a word that came up in their normal everyday conversation.

The Demonex finally left, loped back to the river, jumped across it, and vanished into the jungle. "I guess we can head back," Mora suggested. "It's too late to do any exploring now."

She and the children traveled through the treetops until they came to their first trap. Nothing had sprung it. The family didn't have to leave the canopy to see the covering of leaves hiding the trap from view.

Mora and the children kept going and checked three more traps. The family finally came to the fifth and last trap. This trap yielded results the most often. The family caught more food in this trap than all the others combined.

Mora stopped in the branches and looked down. "That's odd," she murmured. "The trap is sprung, but there's nothing in it."

"What could cause that?" Thena asked.

"It could have been a Crusher," Zaedi pointed out. "The pit isn't deep enough or wide enough for a Crusher to fit into it. One of them could have caved in the mats and gotten away to go crush another day somewhere else."

"We'll probably never know," Mora replied. "You children stay here. I'll go down and fix it. Then we'll go home."

"It isn't that late," Zaedi told her. "I want to go hunting."

"Fine. Just wait until I take Maeno and Thena back to the long camp."

"I want to go hunting, too," Thena chimed in.

"Fine," Mora insisted. "Stay here so I can get this finished."

She dropped to the ground, approached the trap, and started pulling out the support limbs that usually held up the woven mats.

The limbs hadn't gotten broken the way she would have expected. A Crusher stepping on the concealed mats would have snapped the limbs and fallen into the pit.

The limbs rested at an angle inside the pit with their ends sticking out on either side. All the limbs were perfectly intact.

The mats and all the leaves and debris rested at the bottom of the pit. None of the mats had gotten damaged, either. Any creature stepping on the mats would have torn them or at least damaged them.

She pulled up five of the limbs and studied them. She couldn't see any damage on them, either. They looked like they had just fallen into the pit by themselves, but that shouldn't have been possible.

She had arranged the limbs with their ends embedded in the topsoil on either side of the pit. Mora and her children had cut these limbs long enough that they wouldn't fall in. She had to sink their ends into the dirt to anchor the concealment layer securely in the soil.

The trap only worked if the mats lay exactly at dirt level. The leaf cover didn't form a mound to indicate anything out of the ordinary. The whole cover layer sat at the same level as the rest of the ground.

She studied the limb ends and the sockets where they rested in the dirt. None of the sockets showed enough signs of damage to indicate that anything had torn the limbs out by force.

If she didn't know better, she would have thought some person had pulled these limbs out and stuck them down into the pit to ruin the concealment.

She checked the whole trap—and then she searched the surrounding terrain. She didn't see a single human footprint besides her own and those of her children from their last kill here.

She returned to the trap and used her ladder to climb down and throw all the mats and leaves out onto the ground. She climbed out, pulled up the ladder, and started resetting the limbs in their sockets.

She placed them all, stood up, dusted off her hands, and picked up one of the mats to shake it out straight so she could lay it in place.

At that moment, something rocketed out of the trees to one side. It didn't come from the canopy. It came out of the undergrowth on the other side of the trap.

It collided with her and sent her sprawling. She rolled onto her back, looked up, and froze. She didn't recognize the creature above her. It looked nothing like anything she'd ever seen before or even heard of before.

It stood taller than her head and rested on six jointed legs attached to an oblong body lying horizontal to the ground. The creature's head and face came to a taper point and it cracked open long, narrow, pointed jaws to reveal a mouthful of fangs.

Millions of thick, tough, black bristles of hard, sharp hair stuck out of its body and legs all over the place. The creature scuttled toward her on its many legs, let out a high-pitched shriek, and pounced to snap her in its jaws.

She hurled herself sideways to get away from it in time, landed on her back again, and pulled one of her blades from her waistband.

The creature came after her in a heartbeat, but it didn't scuttle this time. It flexed its legs and launched at her flying way too fast.

She sat up as fast as she dared and stabbed her blade in front of her. She didn't take the time to think or check where she was stabbing. She just wanted to destroy this thing—whatever it was.

Her blade impaled its body somewhere, made it screech in fury, and it swung its head around to bite her in half. She couldn't get her blade out fast enough to defend herself.

At that moment, a missile plunged out of the high canopy, slammed down on the creature's head, and smashed its skull into the dirt.

Mora had a split second to see Hangman standing on top of the creature's head before he drove his kukri to the hilt through the back of its skull.

Chapter 11

Mora collapsed back on the ground gasping and choking for air. She threw her arm over her face and groaned in trembling terror as the truth sank in.

Hangman scowled down at the creature at his feet. He didn't recognize it. The children scrambled down from the trees and rushed over to him.

"Father!" Zaedi gasped. "You're here!"

"Are you okay, Mother?" Thena asked. "Did it injure you?"

Maeno took hold of Mora's hand and pulled. "Sit up, Mother! Sit up."

"I'm....I'm okay, my love." She struggled to sit up and put her arms around the little boy. "I'm not hurt. I'm just scared. I'm okay now."

Hangman stepped off the creature, pulled his kukri out of its head, and nudged the body with his foot. "What is it? I've never seen one before."

"I don't know what it is. I've never seen one before, either." Mora struggled to her feet and made one instant of eye contact with him before she looked away. "Thank you so much. I didn't think you would come."

"I had to find you. I've been looking for you ever since that night."

"How did you get down the cliffs, Father?" Thena asked.

"I climbed down with a rope. I'll show you." He looked around. "It's getting late. We should retreat to a safe camp."

"We have one," Mora told him. "I'll show you. We were on our way there when this happened."

The whole family turned back and stared at the creature. "What should we do with it?" Zaedi asked. "How do we know if it's safe to eat?"

"We don't know and we have enough food for now anyway." Mora bent over to pull her blade out of the creature's body. "We should leave it behind. Maybe it will attract other creatures who want to scavenge it. Come on, children. Let's go home."

The party headed off through the jungle. Mora and the children climbed up to the branches. They could travel much faster that way than Hangman expected. The children had developed their climbing skills much more than he remembered.

He had to run to keep up with them. Mora kept up with them, too. He found himself feeling a rush of pride that she had survived and that she had been keeping his children alive all this time.

They dropped out of the trees and approached a cluster of enormous rocks. Mora removed a wall woven out of tree branches, vines, and plastered with clumps of mud. The opening led into a small camp with one shelter built against the rocks.

Mora put the wall back into place. It blocked the clearing so nothing could get in or out except from directly above.

Thena sat down next to the remains of a firepit. It didn't look like anyone had used it in a while. "What do you think that creature was?" she asked.

"How can we know what it was if none of us have ever seen one before?" Zaedi asked. "No one lives in this valley except us. We might be the only people alive who have ever seen one."

"That's impossible," she countered. "They must have come from somewhere."

He squatted across the camp from her. "We should come up with a name for them. We can't keep calling them, 'that creature'."

She cocked her head and squinted up at the trees. "Their arms and legs angle out to the sides like this." She bent her arm over and pointed her hand down at the ground. "We could call them Anglers."

"That's stupid," Zaedi countered. "Anglers is a stupid name."

"Well, what do you think we should call them?" Thena fired back.

"I don't know, but it shouldn't be that." Zaedi turned to Hangman. "What do you think, Father? What do you think we should call them?"

"I don't care what we call them," he replied. "I don't suppose it matters much what we call them. I'm more concerned about fighting them than naming them."

Mora sat down next to him and handed him a bowl of shaved, freshly roasted Gorlock meat. "Thank you," he replied. He found himself studying her. "You seem to be doing well here."

"We're surviving here. If that's what you call doing well, then I guess we are."

"I do call that doing well. You're by yourself with three little children."

"They've been great," she replied.

Zaedi stood up. "I want to go hunting, Mother."

"Okay, my son," she told him. "Be careful."

"Where would you go hunting?" Hangman fired back. "You're barely big enough to take on a Gurlg chick."

"We go hunting right around the camp. We don't go far." Zaedi looked back and forth between his parents. "Should I not be?"

Hangman turned to Mora. "You let the boy go out alone?"

She shrugged. "I did tell them that they needed to learn to hunt and defend themselves and us. How is he supposed to learn if he doesn't try? When does your Clan let them go out alone? I didn't know. He said he wanted to go. I didn't see any reason not to let him. It isn't as though he can learn by having his mother watch his every move."

Hangman shifted in his seat. "I suppose it's all right."

"When did you start to hunt on your own, Father?" Thena asked.

"I don't remember. I guess it was about your age."

"Boys his age were going out alone when I first came to live with the Godless," Mora went on. "That's what made me think it was okay. He never leaves the area. I would be able to hear if he got into trouble."

"You can go, my son," Hangman told Zaedi. "Be careful and make sure you come back in one piece."

Zaedi left through the same removable wall. He returned it to its usual place and vanished behind it. Thena went into the shelter and Maeno started playing with a bunch of sticks and rocks he'd collected. The sun was starting to go down.

"I'm surprised your father let you leave the band to come searching for us," Mora remarked.

"He didn't," Hangman replied.

Her mouth fell open. "Why not?"

"I didn't ask. I just told him I was going. I didn't stay long enough to get into a discussion about it. He would only have dug in his heels and tried to stop me for the sake of stopping me. I wouldn't have let him and then...." He trailed off.

She bent forward and clasped his hand. "Thank you so much for coming. You don't know how relieved I am that you're here."

He extended his arms and pulled her toward him. "Come here. I want you."

He kissed her, but she pushed him away. "I can't."

"Why not? The children have seen it enough times. They already know what we do."

"It isn't that."

"Are you worried about Anava? Are you still upset about that?"

She winced and looked away. "I....I don't want to get pregnant out here—not like this. I still need to be able to move around and travel. I need to hunt and fight all the time to take care of the children. Even if we found a way out of here, being pregnant would slow me down and put us all in danger. I can't do it now."

He let his arms drop. He wanted her, but he could wait. Finding her and the children alive satisfied something in him. He no longer felt that driving madness to keep throwing himself at the world until he did find her.

He leaned back against the shelter wall behind him and watched her work. She called Maeno over and served him food. The boy didn't seem to register that any time had passed when Hangman hadn't been with them.

Thena came back, squatted next to her mother, and scrutinized Hangman extra closely. Thena had changed in the few weeks since Hangman had last seen his daughter. She evaluated him much more closely—almost as though she found fault with him.

Mora brought him back to his senses. "What did you mean when you said you climbed down the cliffs on a rope?" she asked.

"I followed the river to the falls over there. There is no other way down, so I made a rope and climbed down. It took me some time to make a rope long enough or I would have come earlier."

Her shoulders slumped. "I feared as much. I planned to explore the valley and see if we could find a way out. I just didn't want to travel alone through the gorge country."

"There is no other way out," he told her. "I circled the valley three times. I would have found another way in if there was one."

"So how will we get out?" she asked.

"We'll just have to climb out on the same rope—if it's still there."

"That will be difficult," she pointed out. "We would have to carry the children out."

He shrugged. "Then we'll carry them. I would carry all three of you one at a time if I had to."

"Then what?" she asked. "How would we meet back up with your father's band? We can't travel through the gorge country without more men to guard us. We lost people even with the entire band working together. We would be safer here."

He looked away. He had been thinking the same thing, but he didn't like to say so out loud.

Zaedi came back just then. "Did you find anything?" Thena asked him.

"It's getting too dark to hunt." He sat down next to her—across from Hangman. Zaedi studied Hangman with the same evaluating gaze. "What will we do next, Father?"

"That's what I was just deciding."

"Do you know where Shadow's band is now?" Zaedi asked.

"No, I don't know where his band is. I'm sure they've moved on from the place where we got separated from them."

"How would we find them to meet up with them if we don't know where to look?" Zaedi asked. "We couldn't track them over the gorge country. The stone leaves no track."

Hangman had to check himself before he answered. He wasn't speaking to a little boy. Hangman got the sense that he was speaking to one of his initiated comrades of his own age or maybe even older.

"I don't know if we'll travel through the gorge country," Hangman replied. "The rope I climbed down will take us to another valley at the top of the waterfall. The head of the valley connects up to the gorge country. That's how I found you. We may be able to travel from valley to valley without crossing the heights."

"We still wouldn't be able to find Shadow's band," Zaedi pointed out. "They could be anywhere."

Hangman didn't answer. He had no answers to give—not even to himself. He didn't know what he would do, but he would have to think of something.

These children wouldn't stay young forever. They would need more contact with the outside world, spouses, and other men and women to help defend their families. That was the way of the world. No one could hide out forever.

"What will we do about the Anglers?" Thena asked.

"We aren't calling them that," Zaedi fired back.

"We'll call them that until you come up with a better name," she returned. "What did you plan to call them—Pinchers?"

"No!" Zaedi snapped.

"Anglers it is, then—unless lightning strikes and you come up with some other name." She turned away. "I'm tired, Mother. I want to go to bed."

"Maeno should go to bed, too." Mora got to her feet and looked around. She froze when she saw Hangman sitting there.

Her eyes glazed the way they used to when she realized he wanted her. Seeing that look on her face made him want her even more.

Maeno distracted her just then by tugging her arm. She turned away to take him inside. Thena went with them.

"Are you staying up for a while, my son?" Hangman asked Zaedi.

"Not too long."

"You should go in with your mother and the others. You don't want to wake up the little ones by going in later."

"I don't sleep in there. I sleep over there." He jerked his thumb over his shoulder.

Hangman frowned. "Where?"

"There." Zaedi turned around in his seat and pointed at one of the hollows worn out of the base of another rock across the camp. "I don't feel right about going inside and leaving the camp unguarded. I sleep out here every night so I can see and hear if something comes."

Hangman cringed and looked away. "I'm proud of the way you've stepped in to protect your family. You're becoming a great warrior."

"I'm glad you're here," Zaedi replied without missing a beat. "You'll be able to initiate me when the time comes."

Hangman winced. "I'm sure you'll initiate easily."

"I want to become Kral of my band after you," the boy went on.

"I'm not Kral, my son."

Zaedi shrugged. "Shadow won't live forever. Then you'll be Kral the way you were before. We'll all be better off with you than we are with him."

"You're betraying your Clan by speaking about him that way. You should know better."

"He isn't here and you and all the men are already thinking it. You don't have to hide it. No one will find out."

Hangman got to his feet. "It's getting late. You should go to sleep, my son. We'll go hunting tomorrow. You can come with me, but only if you get a good night's sleep tonight."

Zaedi burst into a huge grin. "All right."

Hangman went inside the shelter. Thena was already curled up on a woven mat with her eyes closed. Mora lay next to Maeno talking to him in a low whisper. His eyelids started to droop.

Hangman stretched out on her other side, waited a second, and then rolled over to put his arms around her from behind. He shut his eyes. He didn't want to wait any longer.

He didn't care about traveling with her while she was pregnant. He didn't care how hard it got or how slowly they had to travel. That would be a small price to pay to enjoy her between now and then.

He squeezed her body against him and buried his face in her neck from behind. She tensed and her voice strained just a little more. She grabbed his wrist, but she didn't stop him from holding her.

She didn't stop him when he started touching her, either. He compressed her breasts in both hands and raked his fingertips up her thighs. He pulled her hips back against him and snuck his fingers into her loincloth to tease her.

She never stopped whispering to Maeno, but her body quivered with desire. She wanted it.

Maeno drifted off and she stopped talking to him. Her body responded to Hangman's actions. He knew her too well. She couldn't hide her desire from him.

He eased back and turned her over to face him. Her eyes sparkled out of the darkness to fire his soul. He kissed her, took hold of her hand, and placed it between his legs so she could feel how much he wanted her.

He would take all the time she needed to get ready, but he wasn't prepared to back down—not after he spent all this time worrying about her and searching for her.

She kissed him back and the passion between them exploded. They attacked each other tearing each other's clothes off and grappling to touch each other fast enough. Nothing could stop it now.

Chapter 12

Hangman stood up and brushed the dirt off his legs and hands. "Are you ready, my son?"

"Ready for what?" Mora asked.

"Zaedi and I are going hunting," Hangman told her. "We'll be back later."

She smiled up at him. Neither of them had gotten much sleep last night. Hangman would have to catch up later in the afternoon.

"Have a nice time," she told him.

Hangman and Zaedi left the long camp. That's what Mora and the children called it since they stayed here permanently. Hangman copied what he'd seen Zaedi doing yesterday by removing the wall section and putting it back.

They set off walking through the jungle and then scrambled into the canopy. "Are you sure this is okay?" Zaedi asked on the way. "Are you sure I should be going hunting with you?"

"Why shouldn't you?" Hangman asked. "You're my son—my oldest son—aren't you?"

"I'm an uninitiated boy. Shadow says uninitiated boys don't have any place in the men's hunting party."

"I'm the only man here. It isn't as though you would be intruding on the business of men. Men are allowed to take their sons hunting as long as they do it alone and the men don't try to include the boy in men's business."

Zaedi frowned. "Are you sure?"

"Shadow took me hunting when I was your age. You could remind him of that—since he seems to have forgotten about it."

Zaedi spun around. "He did?"

Hangman nodded. "He taught me a lot. We had a good time when we went out alone. That was long before he became Kral. Midnight was Kral then. Maybe Shadow thought he would never become Kral. He was the same as any other man."

Zaedi scanned the surroundings. "What will we hunt first?"

"What do you and your mother usually hunt?"

"We don't hunt. We use the traps."

Hangman stopped in his tracks. "The what?"

"Traps. She calls them pit traps." Zaedi frowned at him. "You know."

"No, I don't. What pit traps?"

"You must have seen it when you killed the Angler." Zaedi made a face and turned aside in disgust. "I can't believe we're actually calling them that."

"What pit traps, my son?" Hangman insisted. "What is she doing if she isn't hunting?"

Zaedi's eyes fell out of their sockets. "You really don't know? You didn't see?"

"I didn't see anything. I was too busy dealing with the Angler."

Zaedi waved Hangman forward. "I'll show you."

The boy took off through the canopy. He balanced along the branches, jumped from branch to branch, and held on with his hands at exactly the right spots to steady himself so he could move as fast as possible.

Hangman had to pay attention to keep up with the boy. Zaedi led the way back to where the Angler had attacked Mora. The creature lay on the edge of a large clearing, which is where she'd been sitting when Hangman found the creature attacking her.

Some other creatures in the jungle had found the dead Angler and munched on it since yesterday. The ants and Abnormits hadn't found it yet. Part of the carcass was still there where Hangman had left it.

Zaedi didn't go near it. He jumped down to the ground on the opposite side of the clearing. Hangman landed next to him and took a few steps forward to go check the Angler carcass.

Zaedi grabbed him and held him back. Zaedi pulled Hangman back to their original position. "Stay here," Zaedi told him and advanced by himself.

Zaedi dug around in the leaf litter on the ground and pulled up a bunch of woven mats buried under the debris.

He flipped them away to reveal a series of long straight tree limbs embedded in the soil. They lay one against the other to make a framework to hold up the mats.

Zaedi laid the mats aside and pried up the limbs. Hangman stared down into a deep pit studded with massive wooden spikes. He read the situation for exactly what it was. No one had to explain it to him.

"This trap seems to work the best of them all," Zaedi told him. "Mother thinks this clearing is on a line of travel that the creatures follow to get to the river. They pass through this clearing and fall in."

Hangman nodded. "Come with me, my son. I need to go talk to her for a minute. Then we can go back out."

Zaedi looked around in confusion. "Should I put this back? She'll be angry if I leave it open."

"You don't have to. Come on."

Hangman sprang into the branches and waited for Zaedi to catch up. The boy kept casting worried glances over his shoulder toward the clearing.

Hangman returned to the long camp, removed the wall so Zaedi could enter, and then pulled Mora outside. Hangman put the wall back in place to shut all three children inside.

"What are you doing?!" he hissed in her face. "You're using Follower ways instead of hunting for food!"

"What did you think I was going to do?" she fired back. "I've been completely on my own with three children. I had to feed them somehow and I couldn't risk getting injured or killed by hunting. I had to protect myself and them. I was the only thing keeping the children alive."

"You didn't have to rely on Follower ways—and now you're teaching these children Follower ways! How do you expect them to grow up Godless if they see you doing this?"

"They wouldn't grow up at all if I didn't keep myself safe—and them. What do you think would happen to them if I got injured or killed? You can't blame me for using what I know to get food for them when I was totally by myself. I couldn't risk hunting anything bigger. This was the easiest and safest way."

"You can't do it anymore," he snapped. "You'll poison their minds."

She only shrugged. "What difference does it make if we're all dead?"

He compressed his lips. He didn't want to listen to her, but he had to admit she was right. Losing her would have been catastrophic for all three children. They wouldn't have survived long enough for Hangman to find them.

"You don't have to do it now. I'm here. I'll hunt for us."

She threw up both hands. "Fine. Whatever you want."

He stormed away from her. He couldn't remember feeling this angry with her since the first days of their marriage.

She had worked so hard to become Godless, but she never completely gave up being a Follower. He had to admit he may have encouraged her and maybe even used some of her methods himself.

He had let her ideas creep into the way he did things. He could understand better why Shadow reacted so badly to that. Hangman had eroded the rules and conventions of Godless society in favor of everything the Godless despised and shunned.

He stormed back into the camp, got Zaedi, and took him back out. Hangman would have to root these ideas out of Zaedi's head—but that would be difficult considering that Hangman had begun to use them himself.

Hangman's band had used surprise against the Bounty Hunters. Kuvik had set fire to the Bounty Hunters' village and burned hundreds of them alive in their sleep. He had never confronted them in open combat, not even in a surprise attack.

That was definitely not the Godless way. Any red-blooded Godless would call that cowardice—but Hangman hadn't stopped Kuvik from doing it.

Kuvik had explained ahead of time exactly what he planned to do. Hangman hadn't objected or told Kuvik to change his plans.

Kuvik would have changed his plans if Hangman had told him to. Kuvik would have followed Hangman's orders to the letter—but Hangman had gone along with it. He had even helped his men slaughter unarmed Bounty Hunters.

Some of those men had still been in the act of pulling their pants up when Hangman and his men cut them down en masse.

Was that cowardice—to obliterate his enemies decisively once and for all—to free starving, beaten, helpless captives and protect the band from the same thing happening to Godless women and children?

Zaedi snapped Hangman back to present. "Are you angry at me, Father?" Zaedi asked in a small voice.

"Not at all, my son," Hangman murmured back. "I'm exceptionally proud of you."

"Mother says we have to adapt our ways to meet the circumstances. She says you let the uninitiated boys fight with the men to compensate when you didn't have enough initiated fighting men. She says you changed a lot of your ways and retreated and hid from your enemies when you knew you couldn't win. She says it would be stupid to fight a battle you know you can't win."

Hangman looked away. "She's right. Your mother is a smart woman. I did do all of that—and I used her Follower knowledge to help our band. She did the right thing to use her knowledge to take care of you children and keep all of you safe until I could find you."

Zaedi peered at him. "So....will we keep using the pit traps?"

"We won't need to. You and I will hunt for the others now."

Zaedi perked up. "What will we hunt?"

"What do you usually hunt?"

The boy shrugged. "Thena and I usually hunt Gurlg chicks, Abnormits—anything small enough that we can kill without it threatening us. Mother says we shouldn't hunt anything we aren't certain we can kill without getting hurt. She says it's more important for us to stay alive and unhurt—especially when we have enough food."

"I see. Come over here. I think I know where we can find something a little more challenging."

Hangman led the way back to the pit trap. It lay open for all the jungle creatures to see. None of them would fall into it again. They could just walk around it.

The Angler carcass lay on the other side of the clearing in the same position.

"Father?" Zaedi murmured.

"Yes, my son?"

"That....that Angler.....it ambushed Mother."

Hangman froze. The hair stood up on his arm at those words. "What do you mean?"

"It messed up the trap and waited for her to come back. It lured her down to the ground and then attacked."

Hangman turned around and studied his son. "That isn't possible, my son. Creatures don't lay ambushes for people."

Zaedi pointed down at the trap. "The poles weren't broken. We thought at first that a Crusher or some other large creature must have stepped in the trap and gotten out of it because the creature was too big to fall in—but the poles weren't broken. Nothing stepped in the trap. Something took the poles out of their sockets and pushed them into the trap. It looked like a person did it—and then the Angler came out and hit her and knocked her over. The Angler.....it came from over there. It must have been hiding in those bushes—but we didn't hear it. We would have known if it was there. It must have been hiding there before we came—waiting for us."

Hangman turned back to frown at the trap. "That shouldn't be possible, my son."

"I know. I'm just telling you what I saw."

Hangman sat in silence. He no longer cared about hunting anything. A few minutes later, a swarm of ants came out of the jungle and devoured the Angler to the bare dirt.

They also ate the poles, the woven mats, the leaves, and climbed down into the pit to chew the spiked posts. The ants left nothing put the empty pit.

Hangman watched in deep thought until the ants left. The Angler couldn't act as bait for another creature for Hangman to hunt, but he didn't leave.

"Father?" Zaedi asked. "What's wrong?"

"These creatures.....these Anglers.....this valley must be the only place in the world where they exist. Someone somewhere would have seen them. We would at least know about them—but we don't. We don't know about them because people don't come into this valley—not alive. You and your mother and the others might be the only people ever to set foot in this valley."

"And you."

"But don't you realize what this means? These creatures must be intelligent. They must be capable of planning and strategizing in ways other creatures can't." Hangman turned back to look down into the clearing. It was totally empty now. "We have to do something about this."

"What *could* we do about it?" Zaedi asked.

"I don't know, but if the Angler tracked your mother here and ambushed her, they'll be capable of doing it somewhere else. Come on."

Hangman took off through the branches. He had no idea what he would do or even where he was going. He traveled a long way downriver toward the other end of the valley. It was already getting dark when he spotted something ahead.

He had never seen this before, either. That's what gave it away. Whatever these Anglers were, they were completely unknown.

He pulled Zaedi to a halt at a safe distance in the canopy where they could watch the Anglers from a distance. They lived in the trees.

Some kind of armor plating covered their oblong, horizontal bodies, but the armor didn't form an exoskeleton like an ant's or an Abnormit's.

The angled, jointed legs were armored, too, but the joints worked the same as other creatures. The Anglers didn't have exoskeletons.

The head wasn't armored at all. Scaly, leathery skin covered the head and neck. The armor only started at the thorax.

They had constructed some kind of webs in the upper canopy. The web formed a massive cloud of fibers tangled around a big cluster of leaves and branches.

The Anglers went into and out of this web the way Abnormits went into and out of their nests. Hangman couldn't see enough to tell what might be going on inside the web.

He only saw fifteen Anglers here. They came out for a few minutes and then they all went inside and stayed inside as darkness fell.

"What do you want to do about them?" Zaedi asked.

"I don't want to do anything but observe them. I want to see if you're right about them ambushing their prey."

"Won't Mother get worried when we don't come back?"

Hangman found himself grinning at the boy. "I'll explain to her when we get back that I was teaching you what you need to know for your initiation."

"What do I need to know for my initiation? I only need to fight something, don't I?"

Hangman shrugged. "I suppose. Do you know what you want to fight?"

"I keep thinking about it, but each time I decide, I start to think it would be better to choose something else. I can't make up my mind."

"You have plenty of time to decide." Hangman turned back to the Angler web, but it didn't tell him anything. "We should get some sleep. We can follow the Anglers in the morning when they get up and start moving around."

Chapter 13

Hangman and Zaedi crouched in the branches and watched five Anglers move through the jungle. They traveled separately from each other and kept a much greater distance between themselves. No one would have been able to tell that the creatures were together.

They all traveled in the same direction and they all arrived at the same destination. The spot was a clear spring miles west of the river. Mora would have taken months to find it.

Hangman and Zaedi stayed high enough in the branches to keep out of the Anglers' way. Hangman didn't want the creatures to find out that he and Zaedi were following them.

Hangman didn't know what to expect, but he started to get the picture when the Anglers positioned themselves at evenly spaced spots all around the spring. They were the only creatures here—so far.

They must have planned this. They hunkered down in the undergrowth and then fluffed out all the stiff bristles on their bodies to arrange the foliage around them.

The leaves and undergrowth made perfect camouflage—exactly the way the first Angler had ambushed Mora.

Hangman got an extremely bad feeling watching these creatures. He, Mora, and their children were trapped in this valley with these creatures—with the one species of creature actually capable of anticipating and ambushing the family.

Life in the jungle was already dangerous enough. The family couldn't escape these creatures except by leaving the valley.

The Anglers proved him right by lying in wait until four Crushers came to the spring to drink. The Crushers bent their heads low to the water—and the Anglers attacked.

They collided with the Crushers hard enough to knock them over. Each Angler dove for the jugular. They tore the Crushers' throats out while the Crushers still floundered to try to get their feet under them.

The Anglers' speed overcame the Crusher's superior size and strength. None of the Crushers even saw what hit them before the Anglers left them bleeding to death on the ground.

The Crushers roared and thrashed around trying to maul the Anglers, but the Anglers sprang clear, took refuge in the branches, and waited there for the Crushers to die.

Hangman's blood ran cold when he saw that. These Anglers were hands down the most intelligent creatures he'd ever seen.

They coordinated their attack, anticipated their prey, and the Anglers understood enough to get away from the Crushers until it was safe to go back down to the ground.

The Anglers returned to the four carcasses, but the Anglers didn't devour the Crushers. The Angers tore hunks of meat off the bodies and carried it away into the undergrowth before they came back to do it again.

The blood stains around the Anglers' mouths told Hangman that these were the same creatures that killed the Crushers.

The Anglers went and forth until they reduced the Crushers to four identical piles of bones. The Anglers even took away the Crushers' internal organs and tongues.

Hangman waved Zaedi away. They had another two days of travel to get back to the long camp.

Mora made a face when they returned. "Now I know how your mother felt."

"Sit down, Mora," Hangman told her. "I want to talk to you."

"What about?"

"I want to talk to you about the Angler."

"What about it? I told you I'd never seen it before."

"Zaedi says the Angler dismantled your trap to lure you down to the ground."

She looked away. "I don't know about that."

"He says the poles weren't broken. He says nothing could have stepped into the trip without breaking the poles. He thinks the Angler messed up the trap to ambush you."

She squirmed.

"You agree with him, don't you?" he demanded. "Did you tell him that? Did you tell him that the Angler ambushed you?"

"Of course not!" she exclaimed. "When would I tell him? You've been with us ever since you found us."

"Then you agree with him. The Angler hid under cover, waited for you, and attacked when you came down to fix the trap."

She shrugged at nothing. "It sure looked that way."

"I think we should set up the pit trap again," he suggested. "You can pretend to go check it. I'll wait for the Angler to attack you so I can kill it."

"What will killing one of them do?" she asked. "There must be a whole population in this valley."

"I only saw a few. That's where Zaedi and I were these last few days. I went to go see where the Anglers live. I only saw about fifteen of them. We can eliminate them."

She smiled at him and shook her head. "You're wrong. Fifteen Anglers wouldn't be enough to keep their population going. They would have to have at least three hundred—maybe even as many as a thousand. They wouldn't be able to reproduce otherwise."

He frowned at her. "What do you mean?"

"Think about what would happen if the human race only had fifteen people. Their children would eventually start to breed with people they were related to by blood. It would cause too many problems and they would eventually not be able to reproduce at all. No population can survive without a certain number of individuals—a lot of individuals. There has to be enough variation for everyone to breed with someone they aren't related to by blood. That's why the Clans developed the gatherings—so everyone could marry someone outside their own related family band. No one can marry someone they're related to by blood. It causes problems and leads to the whole population dying out."

Now he was the one who looked away. "I didn't think of that. If that many Anglers are living in the valley, then we'll have to leave. We can't stay here with them."

"How will we leave?" she asked.

"I already told you. We'll climb up the rope. I'll tie a sling to the bottom of the rope and climb up first carrying Zaedi. Once I get there, you'll put Thena into the sling and I'll pull her up followed by Maeno. Then you can climb up."

"That means I'll be stuck on the ground to defend the children alone," she pointed out.

"I'm sure you can manage that much. It's only for a few minutes. Zaedi and Thena will be able to protect themselves at the top. I'll send them to the jungle to wait for us until you and Maeno make it out."

She looked away. She didn't argue, but she obviously didn't like it.

She didn't have to like it. Hangman knew what he had to do. The family couldn't stay in this valley with the Anglers. Even traveling unprotected through the gorge country would be better than this.

He turned back to the fire to get himself something to eat. That's when he saw Zaedi and Thena sitting across the fire from him. Each child held a flat rock and scribbled on it with a charred stick.

"What are you doing?" Hangman asked.

Zaedi shot him a smirk. "We're having one of our contests. She can't beat me no matter how hard she tries."

"There's a first time for everything, Zaedi," Mora told him. "Pride goes before a fall."

Zaedi laughed. "I won't fall this time, though." He bent over his stone. "This is my best one yet."

"What are you doing?" Hangman asked. "What contest?"

"They're writing stories to each other," Mora replied. "I taught them to read. They exchange stories....."

"You what?!" Hangman fired back.

"They asked," Mora replied. "Zaedi said...."

Hangman shot out of his seat, stormed across the camp, snatched the stones out of his children's hands, and hurled them against the rock behind the shelter. The stones shattered into a million pieces.

He pointed at his shocked, horrified children. "I forbid you to do anything of the kind ever again! It's bad enough you've gone so far out of the Godless way! You won't do that, too."

"You've used this knowledge yourself, Hangman," Mora told him. "We wouldn't have been able to destroy that ammunition store if I hadn't been able to read the maps to find it. We wouldn't have been able to use the artillery in the northern mountains......"

"That's you! You're a Follower!" He swiped his hand at his children. "We're Godless! We don't read!"

"You could learn to read, you know. Then you wouldn't need me to do it for you."

"Forget it!" He threw himself down by the fire. "I forbid you to teach them anything else." He turned to his children. "And I forbid *you* to read and write ever again. This is betrayal of everything the Godless Clan stands for. I won't tolerate it."

Thena and Zaedi stared at him in stunned shock. Then they exchanged glances.

Zaedi recovered first, got to his feet, and strode across the camp to his hollow. He wedged himself into it, curled up on his side with his back to his family, and rested his head on his arm like he wanted to go to sleep.

Hangman had to look away. He recognized his son's actions for exactly what they were. Hangman had done exactly the same thing too many times for him even to remember.

This was Zaedi's way of dismissing someone he considered so far beneath him that he didn't even deign to respond to Hangman's outburst.

Thena glared at him across the fire. She didn't bother to hide her disgust. Then she got to her feet, stormed into the shelter, and slammed the door behind her.

Mora refused to look at Hangman, either. She went on with her work stitching a new water bag. She had made bone sewing needles and an awl to punch holes in thick hide.

She pulled the cordage through the hide and tightened it before she made the next stitch. Hangman would have liked to talk to her to smooth things over, but she didn't give him an opening.

She was right. No one had used Follower ways more than he had. Her knowledge was one of the things he valued the most about her.

Godless learning to read and write was a bridge too far. He couldn't cross that line. He wouldn't let his children learn to read and write. What was next—that they would start refusing to fight and kill their enemies?

No way in hell would he ever learn to read and write. That was just never going to happen.

Chapter 14

M ora woke up the next morning, left Maeno asleep in the shelter, and discovered Hangman, Zaedi, and Thena already sitting outside around the fire pit. It didn't have a fire burning in it right now.

Hangman bent over a pile of vines braiding them into a rope. "Father is going to carry us up the cliff," Thena announced.

"That's the plan," Hangman replied without looking up.

"You children could help him by gathering vines for him," Mora suggested.

The two children wandered off into the jungle. Hangman made eye contact with her once, thanked her, and went back to work.

She let last night's argument pass. Maybe teaching the children to read and write would just become one of those things they only did because they were alone—like using pit traps to catch game.

Now Hangman was here. He didn't want her doing things the Follower way. She didn't really need to, but she didn't like Zaedi and Thena giving up on their studies.

Mora knew better than to ask Hangman to change his mind. Maybe something would happen later on down the road. Then maybe she would have another chance to teach her children what she knew.

She straightened up the camp and packed up what food and supplies the family had amassed since they had been living here.

She packed the dried food into her shoulder bags and emptied all but one of her water bags for the climb up to the top of the cliffs. She would refill them once the family started traveling across country.

She took her sewing tools, a few wooden bowls, and a small amount of leaf paste she kept on hand in case someone got injured. She kept a small packet of dry Gooji sap for the same reason. She would increase her supply when she found some more.

Thena and Zaedi came back and helped Hangman by straightening the vines and laying them out for him to add to his rope. Maeno woke up pretty soon. Mora helped him and gave him something to eat before the family reassembled outside.

Hangman fashioned two rope harnesses. The first fitted around his chest and crossed in the back to make a seat for Zaedi.

The second would tie onto the rope itself. He would use this to lift Thena and Maeno to the top once Hangman got there.

The whole family went through the camp one last time. Mora put more food into each person's bags and the family left the long camp behind.

Hangman led them on a long trek to the head of the valley. The waterfall's endless roar pounded against the cliff walls long before the family got near it. Mora had never come this close to the falls—not since she first fell over them.

The falls sprayed down into a massive pool that overflowed into the river. The water sparkled crystal blue now. The family could look straight down to the bottom and see Dushags swimming and arching in the current.

Hangman led the way to one of the side cliffs right next to the falls. His rope hung from the highest valley rim.

He had to yell so the others could hear him over the noise. "Remember what I said! I'll climb up with Zaedi, take him to the jungle, and hide him in the trees before I come back for you! Don't put Thena in the harness until you see me look over the side! I'll wave to you to indicate that I'm ready. Then you wave back to me once she's tied in and ready to go! Understand?"

She nodded and pulled Thena and Maeno away from the rope. The three of them flattened themselves against the cliff face.

Hangman picked up Zaedi, swung the boy around onto his back, and hitched the rope into place. The front part of the rope crossed Hangman's chest, passed over his shoulders, and under his arms to cross over Zaedi's back.

The two lower sections of rope formed a seat to hold him tight against Hangman's body from behind. Hangman could use his arms and legs freely with all of Zaedi's weight hanging from the rope.

Hangman yelled something over his shoulder and Zaedi wrapped his arms around Hangman's neck to hold on. Hangman stuck his foot into one of the loops in the rope, swung up, and started climbing.

Mora watched them climb higher and higher. They made it fifty feet off the ground.

She, Thena, and Maeno stepped out from the wall to watch. Hangman and Zaedi got smaller and smaller as Hangman climbed out of sight.

He made it a hundred feet off the ground before a Boultar swooped down from above and made a close pass next to them. Hangman tried to keep climbing, but the Boultar banked and came back for another try.

The creature flew straight at them this time, braked in midair, and swiveled its feet forward to grab the pair.

Hangman spun around on the rope just in time to move Zaedi out of danger. Hangman's sudden reaction left the Boultar grasping at nothing.

Hangman drew one of his kukris, swung the other way, and hacked at the Boultar, but the creature dodged and he missed.

The Boultar reared back and made another dive to try to peck at Hangman. The creature stabbed its beak into Hangman's leg. He kicked out, but he missed the creature that time, too.

Mora watched from the ground with her heart in her mouth. The Boultar couldn't have attacked at a worse time—and she couldn't do a thing to help her husband and son.

Hangman had to keep one hand and one foot on the rope at all times. He could only fight with one hand and he couldn't climb up or down.

Thena went back against the cliff wall and flattened herself against it so she wouldn't see what was happening up there. Maeno must have assumed that was the thing to do right now. He went over there to join her.

Mora strained her eyes to see what was happening. At that moment, an Angler shot across her line of sight. She didn't see where it came from until it slammed into her, knocked her backward, and landed right on top of her.

Its fanged mouth lunged for her face and she threw her arm in front of her for any protection she could get. Its jaws clamped on her arm and she roared in agony, but she couldn't stop now—now with this monster about to kill her.

Her eyes flashed open—and all that pain and adrenaline sharpened her senses. She saw everything happen at once. Her voice echoed up the cliff and Hangman looked down. He saw her right as the Boultar made another dive to stab its beak into his chest.

He barely dodged out of the way. He couldn't get to the ground fast enough to help her. The Angler jerked its head trying to yank her arm out of the way so it could get to her throat.

She floundered to grab her blade with her other hand. She brought it up and stabbed, but the blade glanced off the creature's armor plates.

Hangman looked up to the top of the cliff. He still had hundreds more feet to climb before he made it to the top. The Boultar kept darting in and pecking him the minute he took his eyes off it.

In that moment, a swarm of ants passed across the cliff top heading across the highest valley rim. They didn't see or care about anything happening below them. They found the rope and started chewing their way through it.

A blanket of calm fell over Mora. She was about to watch Hangman and Zaedi fall to their deaths. Then the Angler would kill her and then it would kill Thena and Maeno. None of them would have to worry about any of this anymore.

Hangman stared up at the ants. He barely noticed the Boultar attacking him again. He didn't have time to climb all the way down to the ground before the ants ate their way through the rope. Some of them climbed down it to eat more of it.

Hangman snapped back to his senses and reacted in a split second. He dropped his kukri, plunged his hand into his bag, and pulled out a square of cured hide. He always carried it with him in case he needed it for something.

He wrapped it around the rope, gripped the hide with both hands, kicked his feet out of the loops, and started to fall. The hide protected his hands even as smoke billowed from the rope under his grip.

He dropped fast enough to leave the Boultar fluttering in midair. The sight of Hangman and Zaedi sliding to the ground gave Mora one last rush of hope.

She stabbed her blade again and impaled the Angler through the head. The blow made the Angler clamp its jaws onto her arm extra tight. She bellowed in agony one more time and the creature collapsed on top of her just as the ants ate their way through the rope.

The rope fell away while Hangman was still thirty feet in the air. He landed in a crouch with Zaedi hanging on for dear life.

Hangman dropped the piece of hide and shook his hands out before he picked up his kukri and came over to the dead Angler.

He bent over and saw Mora grimacing and whining in pain with the Angler's jaws still locked on her arm. "Just stay where you are for a minute, Mora," he told her. "Give me a second to get it off."

"Do I look like I'm going anywhere?!" she roared. "Get this thing off me!"

He didn't respond. He got busy taking Zaedi off his back. Hangman told the boy to take his brother and sister to stand against the wall so the Boultar wouldn't get them while Hangman worked.

It took him a few excruciating minutes to wedge his kukri between the Angler's jaws and pry them apart. Even then, the upper teeth remained embedded in her flesh all the way to the bone. The jaws started to close the minute he tried to remove his kukri.

He glanced around trying to decide what to do. He waved Zaedi forward. "Go around over there, my son. Untie your mother's blade and give it to me."

Zaedi hustled over there and did as Hangman asked him. Mora kept bellowing every time Hangman moved his kukri to adjust his grip on the Angler's head.

He pretended not to hear her. He used her blade to pry the two jaws apart and instructed Zaedi to pull her arm away from the Angler's upper teeth. Zaedi did everything Hangman told him to until her arm fell free.

She yelled herself hoarse and finally rolled sideways cradling her bloody arm in pain. The pain blinded her. She couldn't get up.

Hangman let the Angler fall away, sheathed his kukris, and handed both of Mora's blades to Zaedi before Hangman came over to help her up. "Come on," he murmured. "Let's get to the jungle where I can take a look at it."

Chapter 15

Hangman pulled Mora down onto the ground inside the tree line at a safe distance from the waterfall. Blood saturated her arm and kept welling from a dozen punctures on top and underneath.

He uncorked one of her water skins and dowsed her arm to clean it. She grimaced and roared at him, but he didn't stop until he washed all the blood off.

"Zaedi, take your brother and sister into the branches," Hangman ordered. "Don't come down until I tell you it's safe."

Zaedi murmured, "Yes, Father," and he turned away to steer his brother and sister to the nearest trees. Mora shot Hangman a glance and looked away wincing. He dug around in her bag and pulled out her supply of leaf paste. She had just enough to treat these bites.

"You need Gooji juice tonight," he murmured while he worked. "You should climb up with the children. I'll stay down here and brew it for you. Then I'll bring it up to you. I don't want you staying down here."

She grimaced at him, looked away, and choked down sobs.

"You did very well against that Angler," he told her. "You have nothing to be ashamed of."

"Your hands...." she choked. "Your hands....."

He glanced down at his hands. He didn't feel the blisters until now.

"I'll make some more leaf paste while I wait for the juice to boil. You'll need more paste anyway." He wiped the last of the paste onto her arm. "Do you think you can climb up with one arm?"

She wouldn't look at him. She stood up and turned toward the trees, but he saw her fighting back anguished emotion. He didn't have to ask why. He put his arms around her, kissed her on the temple, and let her go.

He worked to start a fire, put some rocks into the coals, and gathered water from the river to make Gooji juice. He ground a fresh batch of leaf paste, boiled the juice, kicked the fire out, and carried everything up into the branches. The children were all asleep.

Mora drank the juice. "Thank you," she croaked.

"You should sleep," he told her. "I'll keep watch."

She only nodded. She kept her eyes open long enough to see him spread leaf paste on his hands. Then she went to sleep.

He stayed awake for a long time. The rope was gone. He had to find another way out of the valley—but he already knew there wasn't one. He'd already searched it trying to find a way in.

He only had to look down at his sleeping wife and children. Staying here wasn't an option anymore. These Anglers seemed to be escalating their aggression—or maybe he and his family had just never dealt with the Anglers before and didn't understand their ways.

Every incident reinforced the need to leave the valley. He needed to find out more about the valley floor and the lay of the land from the inside. He only knew what he'd seen from the cliff rim.

He would have to be careful and avoid the Anglers. They could attack anywhere at any time and they always attacked silently and without warning. Every other creature gave some sound or indication of its approach.

He finally fell asleep and woke up at dawn when Maeno started crying. Hangman tried to take care of the boy, but he arched out of Hangman's arms and stretched for his mother until she took him.

Zaedi and Thena sat across from everyone else and stared at their parents with that serious look of fully grown adults. "Now what will we do, Father?" Zaedi asked. "What *can* we do?"

"We'll go back to the long camp," Hangman replied. "That will be the best place to stay until we find another way out of the valley."

"You were the one who said there was no other way out of the valley," Thena pointed out.

"I did say that," Hangman replied. "I searched the upper rim. There may be a different way out. We might discover it by searching the valley floor and the cliff bases. Did you search the valley floor and the cliff bases?"

"Not all of them," Zaedi replied. "We had to do so many other things."

Hangman nodded. "That's all right. Let's get going. You can all relax at the camp. I'll go out and take a look."

He got them moving. They didn't make it back to the long camp for another two days.

Mora and the children collapsed in hopeless defeat as soon as they set foot inside the rocks. "That was a big waste of time and effort," Zaedi complained.

"It just means we've discovered another way that doesn't work," Hangman told them. "It doesn't mean there isn't a way."

"I want to come with you, Father," the boy insisted. "I can help you on the search party."

"I need you to stay here and take care of your mother." Hangman pulled the bowl of leaf paste out of his bag and handed it to his son. "I want you to put this on her arm morning and evening—and any other time she needs it."

"Yes, Father. Should I give her more Gooji juice?"

Hangman glanced at Mora. She smiled back at him. "I think she'll be all right with just the paste—but keep an eye on her and see how she does. If she starts to deteriorate, you and Thena might have to step in and take over."

Mora laughed. Zaedi and Thena didn't get the joke. They only nodded in their usual serious way and told Hangman that they would take good care of her.

He checked that they had enough food to last them a few days. It would take him that long to circumnavigate the whole valley.

He left the camp, shut the wall behind him, and set off at a run heading straight east. He ran directly across country to the nearest cliff wall. He didn't care where he started as long as he started at the cliffs.

He slowed to a walk and followed the cliffs south toward the other end of the valley. He would have liked to travel faster and cover the distance more quickly, but he didn't want to miss anything.

He walked close enough to the cliffs to see how solid and impenetrable the walls were. He also walked far enough away to see any cracks, fissures, or openings that might allow him and his family to leave the valley.

He already knew he wouldn't find anything. The Anglers would have left this valley and spread all over the country a long time ago if they possibly could have.

They couldn't leave the valley any more than Hangman and his family could. No one knew about the Anglers because no one had ever seen one before. No one entered the valley, and if they did, they didn't survive long enough to tell anyone about the Anglers.

He walked for the rest of the day always heading south. He still didn't make it to the far end of the valley. He really, really hoped that the valley tapered upward into some kind of pass that he and his family could travel through to get out of the valley.

Maybe the pass had some special feature that would block the Anglers from getting through but would allow people to pass through. That would be perfect.

He returned to the jungle for the night and camped in the trees. He put his head down on his arms and went straight to sleep. He was too exhausted to care about anything else.

He woke up before dawn, climbed down, and returned to the walls. He headed south, but his attention always returned to the very southernmost point of the valley where the two cliff faces joined.

They came to a V-shaped chasm. It appeared to have a sloping, curving bottom rising to the upper passes. The chasm looked passable from here. His heart started to lift. This might just work—and then he remembered.

He had explored the southern end of the valley already—from the top. He hadn't seen any V-shaped chasm there. He'd only seen sheer vertical cliffs plunging straight down—exactly like every other part of the valley.

He didn't understand how he could be seeing one thing from one angle and another thing from another angle. He would just have to find out when he got there.

He turned his head to study the cliff walls nearest him. He didn't see a single flaw or opening anywhere. How could any cliffs be that solid—without a single crack or indentation? He couldn't imagine a worse place to get trapped.

At that moment, another Angler landed on him from directly above him. He didn't see any Angler there before. It must have been hiding. It flattened him in seconds and dove for his throat the way they always did.

He rolled sideways, but not fast enough. The Angler anticipated him and tried to bite him. Its fangs slashed him down the back and blood poured from the wound.

He roared out in pain, but fighting this creature at close range set off his battle fury. He rolled onto his feet, spun around, and pulled his kukris to destroy the creature.

He barely got onto his feet before a second Angler launched at him from the jungle side this time. The creature hit him in the middle of his body, slammed him against the cliff wall, and its fangs clamped around his midsection.

The pain exploded his mind apart. He couldn't think clearly. He wrenched around hard enough to tear the creature's fangs out of his flesh and impaled his kukri through the creature's eye socket hard enough to crack its skull.

The creature's jaws fell off him, but only in time for the first Angler to launch at him a second time. He couldn't get his kukri out in time. He couldn't even turn to face his enemy.

The first Angler hit him just as hard and toppled him onto his back with the second Angler still holding onto him with its forelimbs. All three of them went down.

The first Angler shot its head forward to snap Hangman's head off at the neck. He couldn't get out of the way in time. He turned his head aside just enough to stop the creature from crushing his skull.

Its teeth swiped a wicked gash down his face from his forehead, over his nose, and sliced open both his lips before the teeth cut into his chin.

He struck out with his kukri. He didn't even try to aim. The two Anglers' positions held them close enough to bring the first Angler inside his weapons range.

He drove his one remaining kukri under the creature's jaw at the point where its neck met the base of its skull. Another sickening crack of breaking bone vibrated through both bodies and the first Angler collapsed there on top of Hangman.

His arms flopped on the grass and he shut his eyes choking down surges of excruciating agony. He needed help and he was miles away from anyone who could give it to him.

He might already be dying from punctures to his abdomen. He might die from loss of blood before he even got out from under these Anglers. He had to. Mora and the children needed him. He didn't work this hard to get here only to die at the first setback.

Blinding pain blasted into his head and body when he tried to use his arms to push the Anglers off. They weighed a ton.

In the end, he had to bellow out all his injured fury before he could summon the strength to drag himself out from under them. He didn't have the strength to push both of them off—not at the same time.

He flinched again when he yanked his kukris out of the two dead Anglers. He stumbled and staggered away and then took off running for the trees. Time was running out.

Chapter 16

Mora squatted by the fire, scraped the last offal out of the most recent Gurlg chick that Zaedi and Thena had just killed, and put it on the spit to cook for the family's dinner tonight.

Zaedi came over to her just then and held out Hangman's bowl of leaf paste. "Father said I have to put this on you morning and evening."

Mora laughed at him. "I wouldn't want you to disobey your father's orders."

He squatted next to her and applied the leaf paste to the punctures on her arm. The paste had already sealed them up.

Maeno came out of the shelter just then. "When will Father come home, Mother?" the little boy asked.

"He only left yesterday," Zaedi told him. "He has to travel around the whole valley and maybe hunt for himself. He won't come back for a few days at the earliest."

"I'm glad you're here to look out for us, my son." Mora clapped Zaedi on the shoulder. "You're growing up to be a fine warrior."

He glared at the Gurlg chick. "I'm getting tired of Gurlg meat. I want to hunt something bigger."

"Just be careful," she told him.

He changed his tone to a high, lilting sneer. "Just be careful!" He changed back to his normal voice. "You're a mother. Mothers always say, 'just be careful'. Maybe I don't want to be careful. Did you ever think of that?"

She turned to smile at him. Just then, a thump landed outside their camp. None of them could see what caused it. It landed right outside their removable door.

Zaedi spun around. "What was that?"

"I don't know." Mora stood up and drew both her blades. "Draw your weapons and let's go see."

Zaedi drew his small kukris. Thena drew her knife. She had to adjust her grip so she could remove the wall while Mora and Zaedi stood guard.

Mora gasped and lunged through the opening when she saw Hangman lying unconscious and covered in blood right outside the opening. She dropped her blades and rushed him.

She couldn't bring him inside without getting blood all over himself. "Get water, Thena!" Mora called over her shoulder. "We have to clean him up before the blood brings any creatures to attack us."

The children scattered. Zaedi brought over the bowl of leaf paste. All the blood prevented Mora from even seeing where he was injured.

Zaedi left the bowl next to her, walked out of the camp, shut the removable wall, and vanished.

Thena pushed a water skin into Mora's hands along with a square of hide with the fur still on it. Then Thena took four other water skins and raced away to fill them.

Maeno stood off to one side staring at his father in confusion. Mora couldn't deal with Maeno right now. She saturated the hide and started washing the blood off of Hangman's face. A long, deep gash sliced his whole face open.

She left him lying in the dirt by the camp entrance, dowsed him with water, cleaned him off completely, and put leaf paste on his injuries before she moved him inside.

Zaedi returned with a mountain of fresh leaves, a big pile of Gooji sap, and sat down to grind some more paste. Thena came back with more water just as Mora ran out of the first skin.

Thena built up the fire and used two sticks to lower a smooth rock into the coals. Then she poured water into a basin and sprinkled the sap into the water.

Mora laid out a woven mat on the ground next to the fire. She had to get all three of her children to help her drag Hangman over there and lay him on the mat.

"What happened to him?" Thena murmured.

"He got attacked," Zaedi fired back. "That should be obvious."

"What could attack him like *that*?" Thena grimaced at her father. "He's too strong and skilled to get this hurt from a normal creature attack."

"It wasn't a normal creature attack. Look." Zaedi pointed at some of the tear marks on Hangman's stomach. Not all of them had torn out. Some were just punctures. "The Anglers have square teeth. Mother's wounds have the same shape."

Mora searched the rest of Hangman's body for injuries. "It looks like these three are the only ones severe enough for us to worry about."

"At least that cut on his face won't make him any uglier," Zaedi remarked.

Mora couldn't even appreciate the joke. Did the Anglers somehow find out that Hangman was looking for a way out of the valley? Were they intelligent enough to think that far in advance? Was that why they attacked him?

Zaedi worked for hours to grind more leaf paste than the family could ever use. Thena eventually took the rock out of the coals and lowered it into the basin to boil the Gooji juice.

"You children are an asset to your Clan," Mora told them. "I'm really grateful to have you here with me at a time like this."

The two children stared in thoughtful silence at their father. "Will he be all right?" Thena asked. "He won't die, will he?"

"Of course he'll be all right," Zaedi countered. "He's survived much worse than this."

Mora took the Gurlg chick off the spit and divided it into five portions. She set aside Hangman's share for him to eat after he woke up.

She and the children worked late into the night until the Gooji sap cooled enough. Zaedi and Thena got on one side of Hangman and Mora got on the other. They heaved him into a sitting position and woke him up enough to pour the juice down his throat.

He groaned and convulsed when they laid him down. He dragged his eyes open just enough to see where he was. "I'm home!" he husked. "I didn't think so...."

Mora squeezed his arm. "You're home. You can rest now."

He passed out and didn't wake up until morning. The three children tried to stay awake, but they eventually crashed. They were still sound asleep when Hangman opened his eyes and looked around.

He sighed and shut his eyes again when he saw Mora sitting next to him. "I made it!" he croaked. "I don't remember....."

"You passed out right outside the door over there." She stroked her hand across his forehead. "You're still hot. We should give you another dose of Gooji juice."

"Thank you," he husked. "You don't know how good it is to be home."

"Your children helped me save you." She built up the fire and laid the rock back in the dying coals. "Zaedi brought you a bunch of sap and ground you some extra leaf paste." She smirked at him. "He even said at least the cut on your face won't make you any uglier."

He snorted and looked away. "Thank the stars I didn't take him with me."

She didn't ask what happened. Zaedi had told her enough.

"Are you hungry?" she asked. "I saved you some food from last night."

He nodded. "I'm starving."

She brought the food from inside the shelter and propped him up against the wall so he could eat it. He groaned when he stretched back out on the ground and sagged in aching relief.

He fell back into a long, exhausted sleep. She left him there and didn't disturb him. She was just boiling the second batch of Gooji juice when her children woke up.

"Is he still asleep?" Zaedi snapped. "He should have woken up by now."

"He woke up earlier," Mora told him. "You were asleep. He ate some food and fell asleep again. He's grateful to you children for all your help."

Thena frowned at the basin of steaming water next to Hangman's mat. "Why are you making another batch of Gooji juice?"

"He has a fever. The Angler's bite might have some kind of poison in it that infected the wound."

"Your arm didn't get infected or cause a fever," Zaedi pointed out.

She shrugged. "His injuries could have gotten infected another way. He was pretty dirty when he came in. You children should eat your breakfast and start your day. He might sleep for a long time."

Chapter 17

Hangman groaned again when he dragged himself out of a senseless stupor. He raised his head and collapsed back onto the ground when he came face to face with Zaedi and Thena staring at him. "Thank you!" he croaked. "You children saved my life."

"Did the Anglers attack you, Father?" Zaedi asked. "You have the same square punctures on your stomach that Mother has on her arm."

Hangman nodded and dragged himself up onto his elbow. "Two of them ambushed me by the cliff walls."

"How could they know you were searching the cliff walls?" Mora asked from the other side of the fire. "How can any creature be that intelligent?"

He winced and propped himself half-sitting up against the side of the shelter. "They didn't know I was searching the cliff walls. The Anglers use pattern recognition. They saw me walking along the walls the day before. That's how they ambushed me doing the same thing the second day."

"How could they recognize a pattern at the waterfall?" Zaedi asked. "We had never gone there before."

"I don't think that Angler ambushed us there. I think it just happened to be nearby and attacked because we were there at the same time."

Mora sat down next to him and put another layer of leaf paste on his chest and stomach. Then she spread it on his face. His eyes locked on her and he immediately looked away.

"Where did they attack you?" she asked.

He nodded sideways. "Southeast of here. I went straight east and followed the walls south. I didn't even make it to the foot of the valley." He grimaced in pain when he tried to adjust his position. "Something is wrong with this valley anyway. I don't understand it."

"What's wrong with it?" Zaedi asked. "You said you already searched it and didn't find a way in."

"That's the problem. The walls were straight up and down when I searched it from above. You can see that channel to the south. It cuts upward in a gentle slope. It looks like we should be able to get out over there—but we can't. The Anglers would have gotten out a long time ago if there was a way out."

"That's just the way it looks like from here," Mora told him. "There's another valley system on the other side of that channel. The pass rises and then falls to another section of valley. Then that southern part of the valley continues to the walls farther south."

He frowned at her. "How do you know that if you haven't searched the whole valley?"

"We did travel that far south. We thought the same thing—that the channel led to a pass we could use to get out. We only made it to the top of the pass. Then we saw that there was no way out in that direction, so we came back." She scooted over next to him and held out the basin. "Drink another dose of juice. You had a fever last night. I want to make sure your injuries don't get infected."

He drank the juice and she served him some more food. It sure was good to be home.

He didn't remember much beyond the first hour after the Angler attack. He thought he must have passed out in the jungle and died there. Then he woke up here in some version of heaven where everyone took care of him and gave him everything he wanted.

"What's next, Father?" Zaedi asked after a while.

"I don't know, my son, but we have to come up with some solution. I don't see a way to defeat these creatures—not without wiping out the whole pack. I can't do that alone. I couldn't even fight two of them by myself."

"I think we should search the west side of the valley," Mora suggested. "None of us have searched over there yet. We might find a way out over there."

"That would be extremely dangerous," Hangman pointed out. "These Anglers seem to be stepping up their attacks every time they see us moving around. They seem to treat everything as prey. They're attacking us because we're something they haven't seen before."

She smiled at him. "I still think we should search the western side of the valley even if we have to wait a few years for the children to get bigger."

He fell silent for a while. He didn't want to wait that long. If these Anglers did use pattern recognition to target their prey, they would realize pretty soon that the family was staying in this camp.

The Anglers would figure out pretty quick that someone—probably Hangman—had to leave the camp at least sometimes to go out hunting for food.

The Anglers would attack again. How long would it take before they attacked the camp itself? Leaving the valley would become a matter of life and death—in case it wasn't already.

"Tell me more about what you found out in your searches," he finally asked.

She scooted over next to him and drew in the dirt in front of him. "The two mountain ranges come together like this."

She drew two different profiles of mountain ranges, one on the left and one on the right. She exactly copied the line of peaks and passes to where they came together at the channel he'd seen.

He frowned at the drawing. He barely heard her explaining different spots where more waterfalls fell into the valley. They formed different branches of the river that met up with the main channel flowing downstream.

The river passed through the V-shaped chasm he'd seen. She said it kept flowing to the southern valley system. She hadn't traveled far enough away from the long camp to find out where the river left this valley.

"But it must lead somewhere, mustn't it?" she pointed out. "It has to keep flowing downstream—which means it exits this valley system somewhere. We might be able to get out that way if we travel far enough."

"No," he murmured. "We can't."

She looked up at him. "How do you know?"

"I know where it exits and it doesn't exit on the surface. It flows down into a series of underground caves under the mountain and comes out the other side. The river may have even carved out the caves. I don't know, but we can't go down there. Wherever we go, we have to find a different way out."

She slumped in defeat and stared down at the drawing. So did he, but he wasn't thinking about the river, the Anglers, or the way out.

He recognized the profile of mountain ranges she'd drawn. The one on the right—the western mountain range—it was the same profile he'd seen in Butcher's pictures. These must be the mountains where the pictures showed the ancient weapons.

Those pictures had writing on them. None of Butcher's men had known what the symbols meant. None of the Godless even knew what writing was back then. Hangman had only found out after he rescued Mora from the Renegades and she showed him on the maps.

He could have read the writing on Butcher's pictures. The writing might have told him how to find the weapons—if he had known how to read.

She could have read the writing—but one of the men would have had to show it to her—which was strictly forbidden in their band. Butcher forbade it. Shadow forbade it.

Hangman couldn't wait long enough for Shadow to die and for Hangman to take over as Kral. Hangman might never make it back to the band at all.

He saw it all in a heartbeat. Mora was such an asset to the Godless Clan because she had this knowledge. She knew about firearms because she learned about them in the Followers. Red's men found out about firearms from the Followers.

They knew about alcohol. They knew about the Hungry Ghosts. They knew about the Bounty Hunters. They knew about treating illness and injury. Mora found out how to use the cage in the artillery battery by being able to read.

She knew more of everything about everything—because of the Followers.

"I want you to teach me to read, Mora," he blurted out.

Her head snapped up at her jaw dropped. "Uh....what?"

"I want you to teach me to read—and I want you to teach the children to read."

The two children gaped at him with their eyes hanging out of their sockets. "Really?!" Zaedi gasped.

"Where did you get those rocks?" Hangman asked. "Could you get more of them?"

"Sure." Zaedi waved behind him. "The other side of that outcropping is all flaky and falling apart. We can get a bunch of them from there."

"Good. Go get some new ones—and get one for me." He took a deep breath. "I'm sorry I threw your other ones away. That was wrong of me. I see my mistake now." He turned back to Mora. "Could you teach me? Am I too old to learn?"

"No, not at all." She burst into a huge grin and kissed him. "I'm so proud of you."

"Forget that. This is important. I want to learn."

She hustled the children out of the camp. They came back with three new slabs of rock and handed Hangman one. Then the two children got to work charring some new sticks.

Mora erased the mountain ranges. Hangman had seen enough. He didn't need to know anything else.

She started drawing different symbols in the dirt and explaining to him how the letters represented the sounds that made up words. She wrote out the word, 'hunt' and explained the sound each letter made to form the word.

He frowned at it taking this information in as quickly as he could. It all sounded way too simple when she explained it like this. It couldn't be this easy.

Zaedi laughed when she told Hangman that the first letter made an, 'aah' sound. "Everybody knows that!" the boy teased.

Hangman glared at him. "That better be the last time you make fun of me about it."

"You started with A, too, Zaedi, and so did I and so did my grandfather and my great-grandfather before him," Mora told him. "No one is born knowing how to read. Everyone has to learn. I'm sure I know a few things about reading and writing that you don't. You better get to your studies or I can make you extremely embarrassed in front of your father."

Zaedi turned red, bent over his stone, and started scribbling. Hangman caught Mora's eye. She made a face at him. "Don't pay any attention to him. We all started with this. Even I started with this."

She started explaining the rest of the letters and what sounds they made. Then she put some of them together into small words like 'mat', 'cat', and 'at'.

He looked up to find both his children staring at him. Maeno played with his sticks on the other side of the camp. He didn't pay attention to the lesson at all.

Mora wiped out all the writing she had done so far. "Hey!" Hangman exclaimed. "I wasn't finished looking at that."

She smiled at him and wrote some more letters. "This is the entire alphabet. Get yourself a pencil and copy it out on your stone there. Practice that and we'll go on to the next lesson."

Thena handed him one of the charred sticks and he tried his best to copy the letters in the order she put them. He had to wet his thumb and erase them when he made a mistake.

When he finished, she told him to keep going and copy it as many more times as he could fit on his stone.

Zaedi and Thena sat across the fire scribbling away on their own stones. A peaceful silence fell over the camp.

Hangman saw himself doing something so horrifyingly un-Godless, but it felt right, especially because he was doing it with his family. They were all doing it together—and this was important. He didn't realize that before, but he knew it now.

This knowledge could only help the Godless. Every shred of knowledge Mora had ever shared with the Godless ended up helping the Clan in one way or the other. She had never shared anything with them that had ever led to anything bad.

He wouldn't have wanted to go through the last eight years without her help.

Chapter 18

Mora flipped a piece of Demonex hide she'd scavenged from the river, laid the hide down flat on the ground, and piled all the dried meat she had left on top of the skin. She divided everything into four piles.

"We should gather some more leaves, grind some more paste, and collect another load of Gooji sap before we leave," she told Hangman.

He turned around from a place near the shelter where he sat braiding another rope. "Why do you think these injuries are taking so long to heal?" he asked. "My injuries never took this long to heal—and your arm still hasn't healed, either, not even after all this leaf paste and multiple doses of Gooji juice. We should be fine by now."

"I still think the Angler's bite has some kind of poison in it—or some kind of infecting agent," she replied without looking up from her work. "These injuries keep getting hot and puffy. The Gooji juice is working to keep the infection down. It would flare up if we didn't stay on top of it."

He shook his head over his rope. "All the more reason to get the hell out of here."

"We're both able-bodied enough to travel. We have no more reason to stay. We should go before the situation gets any worse."

"Do you have everything you need?" he asked.

"Yes, I'll just take what we have and deal with it on the way. I don't want to come back to the long camp if we do find a way out. We should just leave immediately and never look back. I don't care what we have to go through on the outside. Nothing could be worse than this valley."

"I agree with you," he murmured. "And we should all go out armed and ready for the worst. We won't be able to just walk out of this valley without a fight—against something. I don't believe that for a second."

She opened her shoulder bag and stuffed one stack of the dried food into it. She still carried her needle and awl in there from last time. She'd already packed the bowls, the last of the Gooji sap, and a sizeable portion of leaf paste already ground and ready to use.

She stood up to go check inside the shelter when an Angler dropped from the trees directly above the camp. The creature landed right on top of Zaedi and slammed the boy down on the ground.

Mora spun around and grabbed for her weapons, but Hangman reacted first. He had been moving slowly and wincing in pain a lot, but he didn't now.

He snatched a hefty piece of firewood from the ground right next to the fire pit, took one step toward the Angler, and smashed the piece of wood across the side of the creature's head.

The creature's head whipped the other way—away from Zaedi. The Angler spun around to confront Hangman and he struck without mercy. He slammed the wood down on top of the Angler's head and caved in its skull.

The creature wavered and he struck one last time to completely implode its skull. The creature buckled on the ground right there in the middle of the camp.

Mora rushed over there, dragged Zaedi out from under the creature, and raced around herding her children toward the removable door.

"Everybody get out of the camp—right now!" she called. "Gather your bags! We're leaving right now! All of you bring your bags here so I can put the food in. Come on, Maeno. You can put your sticks and rocks in your bag. We have to go."

No one argued. Zaedi and Thena were already carrying their bags. Mora stuffed the food into them, but she didn't really even care about that.

She made the briefest possible check that Hangman got his bags slung over his injured torso. He dropped his stick by the fire pit and the family walked out of the long camp—again.

They struck off westward without looking back. Hangman and Mora had already discussed the possibility of the Anglers attacking the long camp. Now it had finally happened. The camp wasn't safe anymore. Nowhere was safe.

The family kept going until they came to the riverbank. Hangman, Mora, Zaedi, and Thena constantly surveyed the countryside every step of the way. None of them lowered their guard for an instant.

A few Demonex drank at the river on the eastern side. Hangman found a shallow gravel bar well upstream from the creatures. The family crossed and kept going to the jungle on the other side.

The family had to hike a long way to get to the cliff walls. Hangman stopped everyone there. "How do we search the walls without creating a pattern for the Anglers to follow?" Mora asked.

"I suppose we could stay in the jungle," Hangman suggested. "We can see enough from here and we can travel through the branches."

"I haven't seen the Anglers attack in the branches before," she pointed out. "I didn't think they could climb."

"They can climb. They nest in the branches. The Angler that attacked me dropped from somewhere on the walls and the Angler that attacked you attacked from the walls. They know how to climb and they use the walls and trees."

She squinted at the cliffs. "I don't see anything here. I guess we just have to keep going. We don't need to search an area we've already seen."

"Wait a minute," Hangman told her. "I think we should get closer and check for anything we might not be able to see from here. The way out could be something more subtle."

"What would that be?" she asked.

"I don't know, but I think we should at least check."

"Won't that create a pattern—someone going out there to search and then coming back?"

"I don't see that we can avoid doing anything according to a pattern. We'll all go. We'll all search and we'll defend each other. Then no one will have to face the Anglers alone."

She couldn't come up with any better plan, so they all stepped out into the open. The entire party kept turning around, walking backward, and holding their weapons at the ready. Mora didn't want to get caught unawares.

The party made it to the cliff walls. "We're already here," Hangman pointed out. "We might as well travel south from here."

Mora nodded. The family had nothing to lose at this point.

The party set off down the cliff wall. Each person took turns checking the surroundings including the walls overhead. Checking the walls gave everyone all the time they needed to look for openings and potential escape routes.

There were no openings or potential escape roots. The situation looked more and more hopeless by the second.

"Father!" Zaedi called.

Everyone spun outward and stopped in their tracks. An Angler scuttled out of the trees directly in front of the family, but the creature didn't advance. "What is it doing?" Mora asked. "Why doesn't it attack?"

"That's why." Hangman pointed to a different Angler moving through the undergrowth fifty yards north of the family's position.

"They're getting into a ring to ambush us. All of you follow me! Come on!" He set off striding across the terrain heading straight for the Angler that first showed itself. "As soon as we engage with it, you children break past it and get into the trees. Climb as high as you can and don't come down."

"Yes, Father," Zaedi murmured.

Mora brought her weapons up. This was her chance to defeat one of these rotten creatures before they harmed someone she cared about again. Hangman pulled his kukris. Zaedi and Thena put their weapons away.

The Angler checked itself and even moved back into the undergrowth when it saw Hangman and Mora coming straight for it. Had these creatures ever dealt with humans before?

Mora didn't let herself think that. "Move to the side," Hangman told her. "You attack from one side and I'll attack from the other. As soon as we neutralize it, get up into the trees."

She nodded even though he wasn't looking at her. She sidestepped farther to the left and Hangman stepped to the right.

The Angler retreated a little further. "NOW!!" Hangman roared and charged the creature. Mora attacked at the same time and raised her blades to hack the Angler to death. She didn't care about being merciful or that the creature hadn't attacked her first.

The Angler pivoted right and left trying to decide who to defend itself against. That moment of hesitation cost its life. The Angler turned to fight Mora. She was smaller and obviously weaker.

Hangman hacked his kukri down into the creature's skull, and at that moment, another Angler launched out of the undergrowth right behind Mora. Hangman's warning worked. She already knew more Anglers were moving in the jungle back there.

She ducked out of the way just in time and the Angler landed on top of its dead comrade with its mouth open to bite. Both Mora and Hangman whirled around and hacked at the same time.

They finished off both Anglers, leapt into the branches, and neither of them stopped until they caught up with their children.

Hangman winced a lot when he used his arms. Blood started to weep from his unhealed wounds, but he didn't complain. He wiped the blood on the nearby trees and went back to scanning the countryside.

"We can't beat them by force," he muttered. "We have to outsmart them."

"What about finding a sheltered place farther up the walls?" Mora pointed up at the cliffs. "We could get to one of those ledges and stay there out of the Anglers' range while we find a way to implement your climb to the top."

"How would we get to the ledge in the first place?" Thena asked.

"We would climb. Those walls aren't perfectly smooth. The Anglers wouldn't be able to climb them if the walls were perfectly smooth. We can climb as far as the first ledge. Then your father can lower his rope and pull you children up one at a time. Then I'll climb up. Then we'll do the same thing to the next ledge."

"Camping on those ledges will expose us to Boultars and Ridgebeaks," Hangman pointed out.

Mora shrugged. "Would you rather face Boultars and Ridgebeaks or Anglers? I would rather face Boultars and Ridgebeaks any day of the week."

He grimaced. "You're right. I would, too. I guess it's as good a plan as any."

"The four of us will defend you while you climb up," she told him. "You can take Maeno first, then Thena, then Zaedi. They'll be better able to help me defend all of you if anything happens."

"If anything happens, I'm coming back down," Hangman returned. "I won't leave you undefended on the ground."

She spread her hands. "I can't argue with that. Let's go."

Chapter 19

The family strode back out into the open on their way back to the cliff walls. This was the most dangerous place to be. The Anglers all knew the family was here now. The Anglers were bound to come back and try again.

Hangman jogged ahead of the others to the wall, grabbed hold of the rock, and pulled himself up. Mora and the three children drew their weapons and turned outward to face the jungle.

Mora's eyes darted everywhere searching for the first Angler to show itself. They came almost immediately. The first one pranced out of the undergrowth, tiptoed a few yards to the left, and cracked its jaws to show its fangs. Mora responded by raising her weapons.

Zaedi and Thena both brandished theirs. Maeno still didn't think about drawing his. He was just too young to get it.

That one Angler strutted back and forth over there by the trees. It didn't come any closer. Hangman scrambled higher up the walls. One other Angler came out of the trees twenty feet away from the first.

Mora didn't see any others nearby. She hardly dared to believe these were the only two—or maybe these were the survivors of the previous attack group. She didn't really care.

The Anglers scuttled here and there, but they always kept the same distance between themselves and the family. Maybe they were beginning to recognize the pattern. Anglers always wound up dead whenever some of them attacked these humans.

Mora's eyes darted from one Angler to the next. Which of them would attack first—or would neither of them attack? Would they just stand over there menacing the family?

She didn't dare to turn around to see how high Hangman was climbing. She wouldn't be able to turn around to tie Maeno onto the rope. He would either have to do it himself or Hangman would have to arrange some kind of knot.

One of the Anglers darted a few yards forward and stopped. The other Angler waited another minute before it did the same thing. They went back to pacing back and forth like they couldn't decide whether to attack or not.

"I don't like this," Zaedi muttered. "They're toying with us."

Hangman called down from above. "I'm almost there! Move back toward the wall, Maeno! The rest of you stay where you are!"

Mora still didn't turn around, not even to check on Maeno. The same Angler darted forward a second time and then rushed the party exactly the way she expected it to.

The second Angler reacted too late. The first one went for Zaedi and Thena. They both raised their weapons, but two children this small couldn't fight a creature that big.

Mora reacted on pure instinct and dove in front of them just as the Angler opened its mouth to bite her children in half. She raised her blades to strike the Angler down, but it came too fast.

It tilted its head sideways and clamped its jaws around her body. Her bags full of supplies protected her, but the creature's strength overcame her in seconds. It ripped her off the ground, brandished her over its head, and spun away making for the trees.

She heard Hangman and her children calling out for her. She tried to twist around in the creature's mouth and slammed her blades down on the creature's head again and again. Her blades glanced off its skull and blood welled around the wounds.

She barely saw where the creature was taking her. It took off at high speed into the jungle. She couldn't let it take her away from her family.

The creature's jaws didn't touch her. Her clothes and bags cushioned its teeth. She wrenched sideways, turned her blade around, and stabbed through the back of the creature's head.

The Angler screeched, but it didn't fall. It tossed its head once and thrashed in pain. She had to strike again. She had to land a decisive blow and force it to free her.

She turned her blade in a different direction, hacked down across the leathery skin on the back of the Angler's neck, and it finally dropped her.

The creature buckled to the ground, but it still wasn't fully dead. It dropped her and she fell on her knees. She scrambled away from it and it lumbered a few steps toward her. She couldn't tell how badly she'd injured it.

She dropped her blades, let them fall against the loops around her wrists, and bolted away into the trees. She put enough distance between her and the Angler to clamber into the canopy.

She wilted on a branch in the high canopy and gulped to catch her breath. She panted and sweated all over from the strain of fighting her way free. At least the Angler didn't injure her again.

She looked up to figure out where she was and how to get back to the cliffs. Hangman was over there alone with the children. She had to get back there and help him. Heaven only knew how he would fight the Anglers on his own.

She didn't realize until now that the Angler had carried her so far away from the cliffs. She followed the line of peaks to the point where she'd gotten separated from Hangman and the children. The Angler had carried her for miles away from them.

She looked all around her trying to figure out where she was and how long it would take her to meet back up with her family.

Hangman might have taken the children and fled to another part of the valley. He might have taken them somewhere Mora would never find them.

She had to pay attention when she spotted more Anglers coming out of the jungle from both directions. Some came from her left and headed straight for the cliff where she'd left Hangman to defend the children alone.

These Anglers halted when they came upon their injured comrade. The Angler that had captured Mora kept stumbling around trying to figure out where it was and where it should be going.

It still didn't fall for some reason. The other Anglers stopped there and investigated the creature to figure out what was wrong with it. Mora couldn't really see what was wrong with it, either.

Blood poured from its wounds. She would have thought those wounds would have killed the creature by now, but the Angler still stayed on its feet.

Another parade of Anglers came from the north—from her right. They also met up with the injured Angler, stopped to investigate, and kept going. She followed the direction of their march.

She froze when she spotted a tangled web of fibers in the trees. It looked like a ball of fluff suspended between the branches.

The injured Angler had carried her close enough for her to see through the fibrous outer layer. Hundreds or maybe thousands of eggs packed the web's interior.

A bunch of young Anglers blundered around on the ground beneath the web. A few adult Anglers went into and out of the web nest, but none of them stood guard over the young ones.

The young Anglers only came up as high as Mora's knee and they didn't look nearly as ferocious as the adults. The young ones had short, blunt snouts and no fangs. They actually looked kind of cute—like all young.

The adult Anglers coming from the cliffs continued past the web. They surrounded a half-eaten Crusher carcass lying on the ground and started to devour it in bloody, tearing mouthfuls.

More Anglers showed up from different directions carrying hunks of bloody meat in their jaws. They delivered this food to the young ones, dropped the meat on the ground, and left the young ones there to eat by themselves.

The sight of them fired Mora's protective fury. Her family would never be safe as long as these creatures roamed the valley at will.

She balanced through the branches, left the adult Anglers where they were, and headed back toward the east. She circled the web nest from the north and took up a position at a safe distance where she could watch the Anglers.

She slipped to the ground and tiptoed closer....and closer. She hid right behind the trees where the young Anglers explored by themselves.

She waited for one of the adults to deliver another piece of meat. The adult dropped it, four young Anglers surrounded it, and they started tearing it apart while the adult walked away on its own business.

The young started to squabble over the meat. They didn't see a thing before Mora stepped out from behind the tree. She chopped her blade into their heads one after another and dropped all four of them right there on the ground.

She dove behind the tree and then leapt to a different tree to hide. The Anglers could do their best to find a pattern in that. No other predator would have come this close to their nest to kill their young.

This would be the best way to wipe out the whole colony. No more adult Anglers would grow if Mora eliminated all the young. They were defenseless and naïve. They didn't know about danger.

She jumped out from behind another tree and killed five more. Her audacity started to go to her head. She didn't hide behind the tree at all the second time.

She stormed through the group killing every young Angler in sight before she spotted another adult coming to deliver food. The adult didn't notice anything out of the ordinary.

This situation must have been so out of the Anglers' realm of comprehension that they didn't even look for it. The adult carried the food to the young that were still alive and then left them totally unguarded.

Mora stepped out into the open, strode through the area, and hacked every young Angler to the ground. This killing spree was becoming addictive.

She worked her way around to the other side of the web nest. The Anglers had a lot of young. An army of Godless would have to sweep through here on a daily basis for years to kill all the young—and that wasn't counting the unhatched eggs inside the web.

She didn't care how long it took. She kept striking them down one after the other. She didn't count how many she killed. She wouldn't stop.

She had to stop when an adult Angler dropped from the canopy and landed right in front of her. The creature screeched at her. It didn't look sideways at its dead young. Did the adult even realize what she was doing here?

The creature dove for her and opened its mouth to bite her again. She reacted in a split second, stabbed her blade straight into its mouth, impaled it through the back of the head, and sprinted away into the trees.

It didn't occur to her to climb up into the branches until she'd already run a mile away from the web nest. She paused and looked up at the canopy. She had to sheath her blades before she climbed up there.

She changed her mind when she saw more Anglers up there. They weren't coming after her. They didn't see her—not yet. She kept running, burst out of the trees into a stretch of open ground and ran onward to the cliff walls.

Her one thought was to climb up onto one of the ledges. She needed to rest somewhere while she thought about how to meet up with Hangman and the children.

She had to stop at the base of the cliff to sheath her blades. Then she turned her attention to the rock wall.

She started to raise her head—and stopped again when she saw a cave right there to her left. It angled to the side.

One of the walls jutted in front of the other exactly the way Hangman mentioned that it might. He said the family might see something closer to the walls that they wouldn't see from farther away.

She wouldn't have seen this cave if she hadn't been standing right in front of it. She didn't know if the Anglers would be able to find her in here, but she had to take a chance. She dove into the cave and kept going until the shadows concealed her from view.

The cave didn't have a back wall. It kept going deeper and deeper into the rock until it formed a tunnel. The light coming from outside diminished the farther she went, but she could still see where she was going.

Cracks in the ceiling and surrounding walls cast angled beams of daylight into different parts of the tunnel. She couldn't figure out how this light got inside when she was underneath such a massive pile of solid rock.

At least she wasn't in danger from the Anglers here. Did they even know about this cave tunnel? Were they smart enough to discover it? Maybe they just never saw anyone enter it so they never formed any recognition of that pattern.

She didn't think too much about it. The cave and the tunnel were too narrow for the Anglers to enter. She and her family could hide here while they figured out how to escape from the valley.

She stayed close to the wall and trailed her fingertips down its length for no reason. She would only have needed to do that if the tunnel had been too dark for her to see where she was going.

She could see just fine, but she did it automatically without thinking. Her fingers brushed a rough patch on the wall. She wouldn't have noticed it except that all the cliff faces were made of perfectly smooth rock.

The flat slabs of stone her children used for writing flaked off the rock in sheets without a single imperfection on them. She shouldn't have felt anything rough here or anywhere else.

She glanced over at the surface under her hand—and stopped. Long, evenly spaced grooves scored the tunnel walls. These grooves covered the whole surface, but they didn't travel all the way down the wall from top to bottom.

The grooves marked parallel lines on the wall for a few feet. Then another set of grooves appeared at a staggered place next to the first set.

Dozens of these blocks of lines covered the wall. None of the lines met up with each other.

She stared at the lines.....and her fingers traced their perfectly spaced indentations. They gouged the rock in ways she'd never seen anywhere else in this valley or even in the whole mountain range.

She and the rest of Shadow's band had been traveling through these mountains for three years. The Godless would have seen these scratches somewhere before.

A shiver went up her spine. She had seen these scratches somewhere before. She just hadn't seen them in these mountains. They shouldn't have been here at all.

Her heart started pounding when she realized what she was looking at. This was it. This was the way out of the valley. She had found it—but was she too late to save Hangman and her children?

She didn't leave the cave tunnel just yet. She turned right, picked up her pace, and pressed deeper into the heart of the mountain. She had to find it. She had to. She couldn't go back to Hangman and the children without finding out the truth first.

She turned a dozen corners. She must have traveled another mile under the mountain before the tunnel opened outward into a wider place—a much wider place.

The tunnel expanded into a much bigger, wider chamber. Giant machines sat parked inside the tunnel. They filled the space almost to the walls. Some of these machines sat on wheels. Others used tread-rollers.

A few of the machines had powerful mechanical arms attached to their fronts with claw attachments exactly spaced to match the scratches on the walls.

The machinery would have blocked the way through, but the machines had been parked in the center of the tunnel. They left enough space on either side for her to squeeze through if she turned her body sideways.

She wedged herself around dozens of these machines and rushed from one to the next as quickly as she could. Some sat so close to the walls that she almost scraped her clothes off.

She finally came to the end of the line of machines and took off running the rest of the way down the tunnel. She didn't stop until she saw a round circle of daylight ahead.

She ran toward it......and stopped when she found herself facing the jungle outside the valley. She was free.

Chapter 20

Hangman clung to the perilous hand and footholds on the rock face. He told himself not to look down, but a scream from below made him do it anyway.

He froze in horror as one of the Anglers clamped Mora in its jaws, raised her above its head, and ran off with her into the jungle.

He had to pay attention when the second Angler rushed his children and tried to attack Maeno. Hangman couldn't watch that. He launched himself off the rock, dropped thirty feet, and slammed his heels down on the Angler's head.

His weight smashed in the creature's head into the ground and squashed its brains out. Hangman didn't wait around. He snatched Maeno off the ground and tried to grab Thena, too, but he changed his mind.

"Get to the trees—now!" he ordered. "Get up into the trees!"

Zaedi and Thena took off running. Hangman ran right with them carrying Maeno. None of them stopped until they made it to the high canopy.

"They took Mother!" Thena whimpered. "They took Mother!"

"She was still fighting back when they took her," Hangman panted. "She could have killed the Angler. She might still make it back to us or we could meet up with her somewhere. We can't give up. She would want us to keep going no matter what."

Zaedi and Thena looked up at him in despair. Thena blinked back tears. Maeno didn't even realize what was happening. Did he even see the Angler take Mora?

Hangman couldn't let anything happen to these children. Mora would never forgive him if he lost even one of them. He owed it to her to protect them even if she was dead—especially if she was dead.

He thought fast. He really didn't want to climb down from the trees, but he would have to if he made another attempt to climb those cliffs.

"What are we going to do now, Father?" Zaedi's voice trembled. This was the first time since Hangman had found Mora and the children that Zaedi ever showed how truly young, scared, and vulnerable he was.

Hangman gripped his son's shoulder. "This is what we're going to do. I'm going to take you all to safety first. I'm going to take you up onto the cliffs and find a place where you'll be safe from Boultars, Ridgebeaks, and Anglers. Then I'll come back to the valley and find out what happened to your mother. If she's still down here, I'll bring her with us. If she isn't, then we'll be able to leave the valley and not look back."

Thena whimpered again and a tear streaked down her cheek.

"I'm as worried about Mother as you are, little flower," Hangman told her. "No one wants her back more than I do, but she would want me to take care of all of you first. Going back to the cliff will be dangerous enough." He took off his rope and started to tie it into a harness the way he did at the waterfall. "Zaedi and Thena, you stay here and do NOT go down to the ground under any circumstances. Is that clear?"

Both of them said, "Yes, Father." Neither of the children tried to keep the tremors out of their voices.

He stood up, stole a glance over the treetops toward the cliffs, and spotted Anglers on the walls. They climbed all over the spot where he'd just tried to climb up.

He pulled his head down. "Change of plans."

Zaedi read his mind. "Are they over there?"

Hangman nodded. "They're on the walls. That rules out the cliffs."

"What else is there?" Thena quavered. "We've tried everything else."

"Not everything," Hangman replied. "We haven't tried doing things the Follower way."

Zaedi's head snapped up. "Are you serious?!"

Hangman shrugged. "Fighting them doesn't work. They're too strong, too fast, and too dangerous. We can't risk me or any of you getting hurt. We have to find a way to kill them—a way that doesn't put us in danger. What did your mother tell you about how the Followers kill creatures—apart from those pit traps?"

Zaedi and Thena exchanged glances. Zaedi gulped. "Um...she talked about.....different....you know....booby traps.....and snares....."

"What were they? What did she tell you about? Did she tell you about how they work?"

Zaedi nodded. "Maybe I shouldn't tell you. I don't want you to get angry."

"I won't get angry. This is the best way to keep ourselves alive and maybe find Mother and get out of this cursed valley. Now I'm ordering you as your Kral to tell me what you know. If Mother was here, I could ask her and you know she would tell me. She isn't here, so I need you to do it. Now spit it out. What did she tell you?"

"Well...." the boy stammered. "Some are nooses tied to trees that whip the prey into the air or swing them into a wall of spikes. Some are trigger traps that make a weight fall on top of the prey or send a spring-loaded spike down to stab the prey....."

Hangman frowned. "Spring-loaded? What does that mean?"

"It means it's attached to something under tension—say a band or a bent-over sapling or something like that. The prey trips the trigger and the spring snaps and sends the spike into the prey."

Hangman didn't understand half of what his son was talking about, but that didn't matter because Zaedi understood it. Hangman could just get Zaedi to do it for him—or help Hangman do it.

"Then there are nets that sweep the prey up off the ground if you want to capture the prey alive." Zaedi glanced up at Hangman's scowl and the boy blanched. "I knew you wouldn't like it."

"I'm not frowning because I was angry. I was just trying to understand what you're talking about."

"It isn't difficult." Zaedi looked away. "It just isn't the Godless way."

"That's exactly what we need. We need something that works and the Godless way obviously isn't it." Hangman glanced around trying to decide what to do next and how to do it.

"You know, Father," Zaedi went on. "There is one other possibility."

Hangman looked up. "What is that?"

"You mentioned using the pit trap as a lure to get the Anglers to come after Mother. We could do something like that again. We could set it up to copy some situation where the Anglers have already recognized our pattern. You could hide and the three of us could offer ourselves as bait. Isn't that what Wildling used to do with the Shrikers in the mountains?"

Hangman cringed. "I don't want to offer you as bait, my son. You're my children. Wildling was a grown man when he did that."

"No, he wasn't. He was an uninitiated boy and he pulled down and killed a full-grown Shriker by himself."

"You are not an uninitiated boy, my son—not that kind—and this is hardly your initiation."

"Well, we have to do something, don't we? What will we use as bait if not the three of us? The Anglers are already looking for us."

Hangman fell into a thoughtful silence. Using his children as bait was the last thing he wanted to do. He didn't want to use himself as bait, either, but a few of Zaedi's suggestions appealed to him.

He took his children deeper into the jungle. They stayed in the canopy. It wasn't a perfectly safe place, but it was better than nothing.

He left them there in Zaedi's care and Hangman returned to the ground alone. He collected an armload of vines, went back up into the trees, and spent several hours braiding rope. He would need a lot of rope.

He still had the length he had planned to use to pull his children up the cliff, but that wasn't enough.

Zaedi and Thena helped him. Then all three of them cut medium-length sticks from the canopy and sharpened them into spikes. They didn't have time to do this right, but it would be better than nothing.

They worked until nightfall. They amassed a mountain of good-sized spikes and a fair amount of rope. The work took the children's minds off of Mora's absence.

Hangman distributed food to all of them and arranged the surrounding tree limbs to make the three children a comfortable place to go to sleep. He kept braiding the rope until they drifted off.

His obsessive drive to defeat the Anglers or at least to escape from them—it built into a frenzy. He was the last line of defense. Now he understood exactly why Mora had fallen back on the Follower way. She didn't have a choice. Now he was doing the same thing.

He didn't care anymore. He didn't care if anyone called him a coward or even if they called him a Follower.

He didn't care about anything except protecting his children. Nothing else mattered. Anyone who thought he was being cowardly could try it and see how it worked out for them.

He waited another hour for the moon to rise so he could see what he was doing. The Anglers didn't come out at night. He had eight hours before the sun rose.

He left his children asleep, said a few prayers over them that no Krakelows would find them, and snuck away through the jungle toward the cliffs where he'd tried to climb up earlier.

He'd gotten high enough off the ground to see some of the ledges Mora mentioned. Some of them were more covered than others. He didn't know if he would be able to keep climbing higher from there or even eventually make it to the top of the cliffs.

At least he and his children would be able to camp there in relative safety until he figured it out. They would have one place protected from all the creatures threatening them. That was the best he could hope for in this situation.

He spent the whole night laying snares and traps all up and down the tree line in front of that stretch of cliffs. He covered the whole area in deadly surprises to kill as many Anglers as came after him.

He continued long into the night and laid more traps deeper inside the trees. He didn't stop until he used up all his rope and all his spikes.

He finished a few hours before sunrise. He would have kept going if he had only known enough to construct different kinds of traps. He would definitely have to question Mora about this later—if he ever saw her again.

He got another powerful gut feeling that he *would* see her again. He didn't know why. The Anglers could have already devoured her.

The same compulsive drive demanded that he turn his energy toward protecting his children. He returned and found them all peacefully asleep. He used the last hours of daylight to braid another length of rope. He would need it.

He tied it into a harness around his body—a harness that would allow him to carry all three of his children at the same time. He wouldn't leave even a single one of them on the ground for the Anglers to attack.

He kept an eye on the cliff walls as the sun crept over the horizon. The Anglers had all returned to their nests. They didn't patrol the walls now.

He hadn't seen them climb past a certain height. He couldn't figure out why, but they didn't climb as high as the upper ledges.

He was just eating his breakfast when Zaedi woke up. The boy narrowed his eyes at him. "Father? Have you been sitting there all night?"

"Of course not, my son. I've been out there laying traps for the Anglers."

Zaedi's expression cleared and he nodded. "I thought you would."

"Eat some of your food supplies. I need you to be light when I carry you up the cliffs."

Zaedi started eating and Hangman told Thena and Maeno the same thing when they woke up. Hangman took his time getting the children moving. He wanted them calm, fed, and rational when the time came.

Chapter 21

H angman stood up on his tree branch. "It's time to go," he told his children.

Zaedi and Thena stood up without a word. "Where are we going, Father?" Maeno asked.

"Somewhere safer than here, I hope." Hangman picked up the boy and fitted him into the righthand side loop of the rope chest harness.

Maeno settled in right next to Hangman's body. Mora had carried the boy in this position once he got old enough to sit up and look around. The only difference was that she carried him on her left side instead of her right.

"You two climb down, but don't descend to the ground," Hangman told the older two children.

"Why not, Father?" Thena asked.

"I'll show you when we get there. Now come on."

Hangman climbed down to the ground. He directed Zaedi and Thena to climb onto a branch at his head height.

Hangman picked up Thena and wedged her into the harness on his left side. Her weight made the rope dig into his chest, back, and shoulders.

The tension hurt his recent injuries, but he didn't let it bother him. He channeled the pain into fury against his enemies. That pain would spur him to get this done and carry his children to safety once and for all.

Then he turned his back to the branch. Zaedi had to climb into the harness by himself and fit it around his back and sides so he could sit comfortably.

Hangman adjusted the harness. "Is everyone comfortable enough?" he asked.

Thena and Maeno both said, "Yes."

"Are *you* comfortable enough, Father?" Zaedi asked.

Hangman laughed. "It's a little late for that now, my son. Let's go."

He set off through the jungle. He would have liked to run to get there quicker, but he made himself walk. He had to pace himself. He would need his strength to climb and definitely to fight the Anglers when they came.

He never doubted that they would come and they proved him right a lot sooner than he expected. He headed straight for the cliffs following the same route he and his family had taken a dozen times to get there and to escape from there.

He walked through his minefield of traps and snares. The Anglers must have been following him or maybe laying in ambush for him. His traps started springing the minute he stepped into the area.

Saplings whipped away from their anchor points, zinged back into place, and yanked Anglers off the ground. They shrieked in surprise—and then slammed into the spikes he had embedded where the traps would send each Angler.

Other traps stabbed the spikes down into parts of the Anglers' bodies, impaled them, and left them writhing and pinned down in mortal agony.

Hangman never stopped walking. Deadfalls thumped around him. Ropes whistled and twanged each time a trap sprang. The three children looked around in all directions.

The children gasped every time some hidden Angler sailed into view getting tossed away from Hangman's position.

Hangman didn't dare to look at what was going on around him. He occasionally caught glimpses in his peripheral vision of Anglers whizzing away from him to the right or left.

Their shrieks set his hair on end. Thumps and death groans resounded through the jungle all around him.

"It's working, Father!" Zaedi gasped in his ear. "Oh, my God! It's working!"

Hangman still refused to turn around. "Wait a little longer, my son. We aren't there yet."

The family was getting awfully close, though—closer to the time when Hangman had to make his move by going out into the open. He spotted the edge of the trees ahead. The sun shone on the open ground. The cliffs blocked off everything else.

The Anglers sensed him getting closer to the point of escape. More of them came out to attack. He didn't count how many traps he had laid for them, but enough of his surprises had sprung by now. Traps wouldn't stop the Anglers if they came in force.

He burst into a sprint, broke out of the trees, and rushed to the cliff wall. Another shriek split the air behind his back.

Zaedi yelled out, "Father! Look out!"

The boy twisted backward a split second before a colossal weight slammed Hangman into the wall. He bounced off and hit the dirt with a massive Angler right on top of him. He hadn't drawn his kukris. He needed his arms to climb.

The Angler didn't move. Zaedi's small kukri stuck out of the creature's skull. The Angler stared at nothing through dead, hollow eyes.

Its weight pinned Hangman and the three children under the Angler's body. The creature protected all four of them from more Anglers coming from all sides. They swarmed the area and converged on the family.

Hangman stayed where he was and completely ignored Maeno and Thena screaming in his ears. He pulled his kukris and stabbed any Anglers who came near enough to threaten him.

He concentrated on their heads. Their bodies fell on top of the dead Angler and created an even more impassable barrier for the living Anglers to attack the family.

Hangman's weight crushed Zaedi. The boy squirmed out of the rope harness, but he didn't go out into the open.

He hunkered there under the dead Angler, pulled his little kukri out of its head, and copied Hangman by stabbing as many other Anglers as his short arms could reach.

He and Hangman only had to keep this up for a few minutes before they killed enough Anglers to cover and protect themselves completely.

"Hey!" Hangman yelled at Thena and Maeno. "We're okay! We're safe for now! You don't need to cry! We're protected."

They stopped howling and bellowing, but they didn't stop crying. Both of them whimpered and looked around in terror at the dead bodies blocking them in. Only a few hints of light squeaked between the Anglers' bodies to gleam into the hollow underneath.

Zaedi squatted on the ground. "What do we do now, Father? We can't get to the cliffs with all these Anglers around."

"We'll wait for nightfall when they go back to their nest." Hangman shot his son a grin on the side. "That was well done, my son. That was excellent. You saved the whole family."

Zaedi blushed and looked away. He opened his mouth, probably to tell Hangman that it was nothing.

The boy froze with his mouth open and stared out at the field. "Look!" he whispered.

Hangman had to twist all the way over onto his side to see what Zaedi was looking at.

Hangman's heart stopped when he saw all the Anglers fighting over something out in the field. At least twenty of them scuttled, screeched, and scrambled trying to get to something out there.

Mora balanced standing on top of one of the Angler's backs. The creature tried to rear to throw her off, but she stayed where she was and rode the thing standing fully upright.

She stabbed one of her blades down into the back of its skull and rode it to the ground. All the other Anglers tried to clamber on top of that one Angler to get to her. They climbed up its body as it collapsed underneath her.

She took that opportunity to step or leap onto the next Angler and repeated the process. She balanced there while it tried in every way to throw her off into its waiting jaws—until she stabbed that one, too.

She worked her way through the whole crowd of Anglers. They couldn't get to her no matter what they did. Their own efforts to attack her played right into her strategy.

Hangman swallowed hard. "How is she doing this?" Zaedi whispered.

Hangman could only shake his head in amazement. He'd never seen her do anything as balls-out audacious as this.

She seemed to understand how over-the-top gutsy this move was. She clenched her teeth in deadly fury, snarled down at the Anglers, and roared out at them when she plunged her blade into their skulls. She struck again and again without stopping.

Maeno and Thena both stopped crying when they saw what she was doing. All four watched her slaughter the Anglers one after another.

Hangman couldn't lie here and let her do all the work. He pried himself off the ground, heaved the dead Anglers off, and his children scampered out. Thena and Maeno stayed near the cliff face.

Zaedi tried to lift the dead Anglers off, but Hangman had to do the work himself in the end. He crawled out, told Zaedi to stay here and defend his brother and sister, and Hangman ran out into the field.

Mora had already done most of it herself. Hangman helped her finish off the last six Anglers. They were all too busy trying to get to her. They didn't see him coming before he killed them from behind.

She jumped off the last Angler and almost collapsed against him. "Are you all right?!" he yelled. "Did that Angler injure you?!"

She completely ignored his question. "You have to come with me right now, Hangman! I don't have time to explain! I found the way out! You have to come with me right now!"

She didn't give him a chance to ask any questions or even acknowledge her victory. She tore away from him, raced across the field, and snatched Maeno off the ground.

Mora tried to lift Thena, too, but Mora couldn't carry both of them. Hangman picked up Thena instead.

Mora hustled everyone away, but the family only made it a dozen yards before more Anglers came out of the jungle.

Mora practically threw Maeno on the ground and ripped Thena out of Hangman's arms. "Run!" Mora bellowed. "Run down the cliff!

You'll see a cave! Take them, Zaedi! Run down the cliff to the cave! Go!"

Hangman didn't ask any questions. She obviously knew what she was talking about. He pulled his kukris, turned backward, and braced himself to make his last stand.

Mora did the same thing, but she grabbed his arm and pulled him backward even as the Anglers moved in. She wouldn't let him slow down for an instant. She kept yelling at him to keep moving no matter what.

Twenty Anglers fanned out to surround the pair. Hangman would have liked to see where his children were, but he didn't dare to take his eyes off the Anglers.

They picked up speed crossing the field and then charged in one coordinated pack. He stopped where he was and dug his feet into the soil to take the impact, but Mora didn't let him.

She tackled him with all her weight and sent him bowling across the hard dirt. He tumbled over and over and tried to shake her off so he could fight the Anglers.

He finally succeeded in untangling himself from her. He vaulted to his feet—and realized where he was.

He and Mora stood behind a stone wall angled outward from the cliff face—or rather a narrow fissure cut behind one section of stone to form a separate wall section between the cliff and the outside world.

That wall blocked the Anglers from slaughtering Hangman and Mora right there and then, but the wall only blocked the creatures for an instant. They figured out all too soon where their prey was.

Mora attacked Hangman, shoved him sideways, and pushed him into a tunnel running under the mountain.

The children met them there, grabbed their parents, and pulled Mora and Hangman into a run. "Run!" she yelled. "Keep going! Don't stop! Come on, Hangman! Hurry!"

He tried to see what the Anglers were doing. They swarmed around the wall and found the space behind it, but the Anglers couldn't get inside.

Those few seconds gave the family just enough time to put some distance between them and the Anglers. The Anglers stretched their legs into the tunnel, but the creatures couldn't get inside.

Their feet and legs scratched all over the stone surface as they tried in vain to claw their way inside. The Anglers shrieked their heads off, but they couldn't fit into such a small space. The family was finally safe.

Mora grabbed Maeno off the ground and took off with him at her top speed. Hangman snatched Thena and then scooped up Zaedi, too. The Anglers' enraged screeches echoed down the tunnel.

Hangman turned a corner and skidded to a halt when he came face to face with a bunch of ancient machinery. He'd seen plenty of it in the ancient cities.

Seeing it here in such an unlikely context startled him into stopping in his tracks. What in the name of God was all of this doing down here of all places?

Mora didn't give him a chance even to understand what was happening. She grabbed him, yanked him forward, and shoved him by main force between one of the machines and the tunnel wall.

The children could fit into the space much more easily. Hangman realized in an instant what Mora was trying to do.

He shoved himself along the nearest machine. He had to cram himself between the enormous thing and the hard, rough stone wall.

He eventually made it to an open space behind the machine, but more and more and more of these things blocked the whole tunnel.

He scraped himself a little farther back, dragged her into the tight space, and they kept going to the other end.

Mora collapsed back against the wall gasping, panting, and sweating. She trembled all over. Hangman stared back down the tunnel at the Anglers for a minute. They still clawed at the rock face trying to get into the tunnel.

Then he turned to stare at her. She never ceased to amaze him with her courage and ingenuity. She wasn't the strongest woman in the Godless Clan or the best fighter by a million miles. He still wasn't even convinced that she was Godless.

She was hands down the bravest woman he had ever met. She was as brave as any of his relatives. She was a thousand times braver than some men he could think of.

She was the one who did all of this. She was the one who got the family out of here. She had saved her children and now she had saved all of them—again.

She swallowed hard and her face spasmed with anguished emotion—even now at the hour of her greatest victory—and no one on the outside would ever find out that she did all of this.

Hangman would never tell anyone. This victory somehow seemed too important to broadcast it to the world.

A select few of his closest friends and relatives knew who and what she was. Viking fell into that category—Viking, Cross, Red's men, and Hammer's band. They all knew and respected Mora. It was impossible not to.

She turned to face Hangman, but she barely saw him at all. Her mind was completely gone with anxiety and nervous tension. She waved him away and said something, but he couldn't hear her over the Anglers' constant shrieking.

Mora followed him to the other end of the machinery, left him there, and went to retrieve the children from their hiding place. They cowered under that first machinery and hadn't gone any further.

She squatted down and then had to crawl in there to convince the children to come out to her. She gathered Maeno in her arms, hugged all three children, and then bent low next to their ears to tell them what to do. She pointed at the machines behind that first one.

The family spent the next ten minutes scooting past one machine after another. The ancients must have parked fifty machines of different kinds down here.

The family eventually came out the other side of the machines and reentered the open tunnel. Mora's expression cleared. She started to smile, but her features kept quivering all over and she fought back tears.

She wouldn't stop smiling up at Hangman and then looking ahead toward a circle of light in the distance.

The family kept walking and eventually came to the end of the tunnel where it opened into another valley. Sunshine bathed the jungle ahead.

Mora led the family out into the open, burst into tears, and fell on her knees hugging all her children in a rush of relief and happiness.

Hangman couldn't stay away from them. He went over there and wrapped his arms around all of them. The nightmare was over. They made it. They escaped and now the world lay open for them to finally get away. They were free.

Chapter 22

M ora stood up, wiped the tears off her cheeks, and glanced around. "Well, here we are. We're out of the valley."

Zaedi grabbed her hand and beamed up at her. "You did it, Mother! You found the way out!"

She smiled at him fighting back tears. "Yeah! We made it! We never have to go back."

Thena rushed her from the side and hugged Mora around the waist. "We thought you were dead, Mother! We thought the Anglers ate you!"

Mora burst into laughter mixed with tears. "I thought so, too, my love. I thought I was finished."

She turned to look up at Hangman. He wouldn't stop staring at her.

He dove in and kissed her the minute they made eye contact. He pulled away, but he kept his arm around her waist.

"Let's get into the jungle and make camp in the trees," he decided. "I don't want to go anywhere for a while. Let's just stay here for a day or two and think about what we want to do next. We don't have to think about anything else or protect ourselves from the Anglers. Come on. We need to take a break and rest."

No one argued. Thena took one of Mora's hands and Maeno took the other. She had never been so happy to just walk through the jungle with her children. Everything about the world looked so unbearably beautiful all of a sudden.

The children smiled more than she could remember in a long time. They kept beaming up at her and bursting out in excited laughter. This was the happiest any of them had ever been.

Hangman didn't join in the laughter, but he kept catching her eye. His expression overflowed with admiration and understanding. He didn't have to say a word.

The family climbed up into the trees. Everyone settled down and relaxed in ways they hadn't allowed themselves to in a long time.

"The world seems so much safer, doesn't it?" she remarked. "All the same creatures are still out there waiting to kill us, but the world feels so safe all of a sudden. It feels comforting and even welcoming."

"I feel the same thing," Hangman replied. "This world feels so easy compared to life in the valley."

"I won't be in any hurry to go back and see the Anglers again," Zaedi remarked.

Hangman stroked the boy's hair and smiled at him for the first time. "You did excellently, my son. I've never been prouder of you."

Zaedi looked away and pretended to scan the countryside. "Where are we? How do we meet up with Shadow's band after this?"

"I don't know where we are," Mora replied. "I suppose we'll need to explore around and find out before we decide where to go and what to do."

"I think we should go back to the eastern gorge camp. Shadow's band was heading there originally. He was still trying to get there when we got separated. He had to change his course a few times to avoid enemy Clans, but he'll keep trying to go back there. We can meet up with him there."

"Then the question becomes which direction we go to get there," Mora went on. "

"We'll start by heading south," he replied. "We're bound to return to familiar territory there, but I'm in no hurry to leave."

She smiled at him and then blushed when she saw the way he was looking at her. She concentrated on her children instead—and just enjoying how relaxed and unhurried this moment felt.

Everything about this world felt easy. The journey ahead would be long and dangerous, but even that felt easy compared to dealing with the Anglers.

Everyone took out their food supplies and ate together. No one talked about how to protect the family from who or what might be hunting them right now.

The family lounged in the branches until Mora heard a Krakelow scratching through the canopy not far away. It traveled at an angle heading away from the family.

Mora, Hangman, and Zaedi all sat up to listen. Then they exchanged glances and laughed. They were back in the world full of all the dangers they knew so well. The three of them could go back to worrying about getting attacked by something else now.

The sun eventually went down. It sank toward the left side of the valley—the western side. This valley must lie in an east-west direction.

"This valley runs parallel to the Angler valley," Hangman remarked. "We can just follow it south. That makes it easy."

"How is it easy?" Zaedi asked. "We have to cross all that country to return to Shadow's territory."

Hangman shrugged. "I can think of worse places to travel than this valley. At least we'll be in the jungle and not walking along those narrow gorge paths. That was a recipe for disaster. At least here we can take refuge in the trees if we need to. We can hunt and find water here. As soon as we leave this valley, we should find another one like it that runs north to south. We should stay in valleys full of jungle. I don't want to go back up on the mountainsides."

"I agree with you," Mora replied. "At least the canopy protects us from Boultars and Ridgebeaks. We were totally exposed up there."

"How far south is the east gorge camp, Father?" Zaedi asked. "How far would we have to travel?"

"I'm not sure because I only visited the gorge camp a few times when I was your age. I remember how to get to it from our former long camp, but I don't know how to find it from the north." He frowned to himself. "That may be why Shadow stayed in the mountains for so long. He may not have known how to find the east gorges."

Zaedi gasped. "You spoke against your Kral!"

"I'm not speaking against him. I'm explaining one reason he may not have returned to the east gorges sooner. He may have diverted one too many times and gotten lost. It could happen to anyone." Hangman looked away. "That may explain why he got so bad-tempered these last few years. He may have been terrified of anyone finding out."

"Do you think anyone would have done anything if they did find out?" Mora asked.

He shrugged. "Maybe not. It wasn't as if anyone could get us off the mountainsides. We were stuck there until we came to another valley system—or I should say no one would have done anything about that. Someone may have stuck their neck out about other things, though."

Mora let the subject drop. Thena changed it by asking for more food. Mora gave it to her.

"I should hunt before we leave here," Hangman remarked. "We should camp here for a few days, take it easy, and resupply before we head across the valley."

"I want to gather some more Gooji sap," Mora told him. "You and I should keep taking the juice until these wounds heal."

"We have enough time for that." He reclined back in the branches. "I could go to sleep right now."

"Go ahead."

Zaedi laughed. "I'll guard the women and children, Father."

Hangman smirked at him, rested his head against the tree trunk, and shut his eyes. The three children took it easy for the rest of the day. Zaedi and Thena started playing their spelling game.

Their noise and laughter woke up Hangman—if he really had been asleep. He raised his head and listened to them for a while, but he didn't interject. He wasn't anywhere near ready to start spelling their words.

Mora saw him watching them. "Do you want to go over some of it now? We aren't doing anything else."

"We might as well." He looked around. "We don't have any stones to write on."

"You can write on the tree trunk. Here." She took out one of her blades and used it to cut a square sheet of bark off the trunk behind her. She unrolled it and then took one of the children's charred pencils out of her bag. "You can use this."

"So what do you want me to do?" he asked. "Please don't say I have to copy the alphabet again."

She laughed at him and started writing out some more very simple words like, 'in', 'on', 'and', and 'to'.

He copied them all, but he got stuck when she tried to explain the difference between, 'to', 'two', and 'too'.

He glared at her. "This makes no sense at all! Why can't they just use one word for all three?"

She shrugged and spread her hands. "I don't make the rules. Sometimes they use different words for different meanings. Other times they use the same spelling for two different meanings....and then there are words like 'plane' and 'plain'."

He threw down his pencil hard enough to make it bounce off the branch and fly away into the undergrowth. "This is stupid! No one can learn this nonsense."

She scooted over next to him and put her arm around him. "Don't give up. It isn't the easiest language to learn. You've been doing so well."

"Don't worry, Father," Zaedi told him. "I wanted to quit when she told me about ......

Hangman glared at his son and then at the words in front of him. "Tell me again why I agreed to do this."

"You agreed to do it so you could get good enough to beat me and Thena in a spelling and writing contest," Zaedi told him. "You know Mother is going to give you special information she won't give us. She'll make sure you get good enough to beat us."

Hangman didn't stop scowling at everyone. Mora had to stop herself from laughing at him.

He stood up and stormed off, but he only did it to climb down the tree and retrieve the pencil. He came straight back, bent over his bark sheet, and started copying the words she gave him to copy. He refused to look at anyone for the rest of the evening.

Chapter 23

Hangman didn't look up from his work, not even when Mora gave him new words and a few simple sentences to work on. He waited until the children all fell asleep before he put his bark and pencil aside.

"You're doing very well," she told him. "I'm proud of you."

"Tell me about the country to the south where you come from."

She spun around. "What? Why do you want to know that?"

"I'm thinking about what you said about the cities and the maps. You know that country better than we do. What else did you see down there?"

"Um...there's nothing there except a bunch of cities."

"How did you know about the Renegade's Jeweled River installation? You knew they had....what did you call it? Was it tarmac? You said they had flying machines and all kinds of things. Did you ever see anything like that?"

"Not in person. I saw pamphlets of it in the cities—in the bookstores. We always go to the bookstores to see if we can find anything new. That's where I saw it."

"What's a pamphlet?" he asked.

She waved her hands around and then made a rectangular shape with her thumb and forefinger. "It's a folded piece of paper—like this.

It unfolds to a sheet about this big and folds up into a little booklet about this big. It usually has glossy pictures and writing that tell you about whatever the pamphlet wants to tell you about. The gloss on the pictures preserved the paper better than other kinds of written material produced in ancient times. A lot of the stores in ancient cities had pamphlets announcing that the military was recruiting people to come and join and fight in the army. The pictures show some of the big artillery pieces, aircraft, bases, buildings—it just depends on what they're advertising."

Hangman narrowed his eyes at her. "So what does the writing say?"

"Most of it just tells you what they're offering if you join and sometimes what you have to do to get in."

"So none of the writing tells you where the artillery pieces, aircraft, and buildings are?"

Now she was the one who frowned at him. "Why do you want to know that?"

"I'm curious about where you learned all of this. Did you learn all of that by reading the pamphlets?"

"There and other places. The Followers read everything they can get their hands on about ancient times. We already knew they had giant militaries with advanced technological weapons, vehicles, aircraft, and enormous bases with thousands of soldiers—sometimes even hundreds of thousands of soldiers. We saw pictures of some of it in books and other places, but the glossy pamphlets are the best preserved and they're in color and everything. The military went to great lengths to make the pictures look extra appealing and the weaponry look extra powerful—for obvious reasons."

He looked away in another direction.

"I don't understand why you want to know all of that," she went on.

"Just answer my question. Do the pamphlets tell you where the equipment is?"

"Sometimes. Sometimes the picture will have a caption telling you where the picture was taken. The caption tells which base the artillery or the aircraft are stationed at and which model of gun or aircraft it is."

"And you never saw one of these bases in the south country?"

She gulped. "Why are you asking me that?"

"Did you see it or not?"

"No!" she gasped. "I told you that."

He looked away again. She didn't engage him in conversation again. He hadn't questioned her like this since Zyria's execution.

Mora didn't see how knowing about the base could possibly make him mad at her. She didn't understand any of this.

He remained silent after that, but when it came time to go to sleep, he pulled her close to him. "Are you mad at me?" she asked.

"Of course not. I'm exceptionally pleased with you for getting us out of the valley. Why would I be mad at you?"

"I just wondered. You were so harsh about the bases to the south."

"Never mind." He kissed her on the side of the head, but he didn't escalate it beyond that. "I'm very proud of you. We'll leave here tomorrow and travel west."

"It's too bad we don't have map of this country," she remarked.

"I was just thinking the same thing earlier."

She settled into his arms, now that she knew he wasn't upset with her.

He hugged her tighter. "You're an asset to your Clan," he murmured into her hair.

"I'm glad the children will be going back to the band. I was really worried about what would happen to them if we stayed isolated for too long."

"Zaedi is sure growing up fast," he remarked. "I knew he had spirit. I didn't know he would turn out like this."

She nudged him. "He takes after his father."

"That's what worries me."

She laughed at him. "Now you know what your parents went through."

"Maeno is likely to be a terror, too, with Zaedi as an example in front of him."

"Cross isn't a terror," she pointed out. "He's so steady compared to you. Bantam seems very level-headed, too."

"You're right. Cross is a fine man. I'm glad he didn't turn out like me. He went his own way and became something great."

She lowered her voice to a murmur. "Do you ever think about going back to Hammer's band instead of Shadow's?"

"I think about it, yes."

"And?" she asked. "You've clearly decided to continue with Shadow."

"He needs me more than Hammer does. Shadow needs to see me supporting him the way Butcher needed people to see Shadow supporting him. Butcher could never have stayed Kral as long as he did if Shadow hadn't supported him."

"But the band would have been better off with Shadow as Kral. Isn't that the whole point—that the Kral sets the band's wellbeing above everything else?"

He shrugged. "Shadow would have had to betray his own brother if he didn't support Butcher. I understand so much better now why

Shadow kept silent for so long. I could never betray Shadow by abandoning him when he needs me."

"But he would never find out that you abandoned him. He would assume that you died in this wilderness or that something else happened to you. He wouldn't find out that you went over to Hammer."

"I couldn't go over to Hammer. In the first place, I could never become Hammer's subordinate. My presence in his band would naturally lead to the same conflicts I'm already having with Shadow. Hammer would become defensive of his position. He would hate me for being there—and all his men would feel obligated to treat me as their Kral—the way they treated me as their Kral all their young years."

Now she was the one who shrugged. "I suppose you're right."

"And for another thing, Shadow could very well find out that I was living with another band. He would see me when our children went to the gathering or somewhere else like that—or he might just hear about it from someone else. I would have to explain why I didn't come back to him. I could lie and say I didn't know where he was—which might be true—but it would still raise questions and suspicions in his mind. God knows he has enough of them already."

"But going back to him won't be totally problem-free, either, will it?" she pointed out. "He already suspects you and resents you. You coming back will only turn him against you all over again. It could get even worse."

He sighed and looked away while she reclined in his arms. "I'm certain that it will, but that is my home family band. My mother, brothers, and cousins are all in that band. I have to go back. It's the only band I'll ever truly belong to. Besides, something could happen to him and I would become Kral. That really would be the best thing for the band. All the men know it. I would be betraying them, too, if I didn't go back."

She sighed and stared off into the night. "I suppose so. The children need people to grow up with, too. Heaven knows Zaedi needs other men and other boys. He worships you, but he needs more. They all do."

"Of course. We don't live in bands by accident." He looked down at her and kissed her on the cheek again. "You should go to sleep."

"So should you. Don't stay up all night."

"I won't. We can go to sleep together. Then neither of us can pretend that we stayed up while the other slept."

She laughed and they settled down together in the branches. He curled in behind her and wrapped his arms around her. They listened to the night noises for a while. Everything sounded peaceful and right in the jungle.

Mora drifted off with those sounds in her ears. She could finally put the Angler valley behind her and move on to the next part of her life.

Chapter 24

Hangman cast a glance to the right and left and then behind him. His ears picked up all the usual jungle noises. He even saw Crushers and Gorlocks stomping through the dense undergrowth. Boultars and Ridgebeaks wheeled in the sky.

He didn't see any Anglers out here. They couldn't have escaped the valley, but he still found himself checking for them everywhere. He kept expecting one or more of them to pounce on him and annihilate his family even here.

Mora and the children acted a lot jumpier now, too. Not even spending three days in their tree camp outside the tunnel could erase their recent ordeal so easily.

Hangman had spent the days hunting and preserving the meat for their journey. Mora and Zaedi had gathered a much bigger reserve of Gooji sap and Mora dosed both herself and Hangman before they left to continue on their journey.

Zaedi and Thena kept a close watch on the surrounding countryside, too. Both of them had become even more watchful than they had been when Hangman found them in the valley.

Both children moved their hands to their weapons much more quickly than they needed to, even when they saw some creature moving away from the family or not near enough to threaten anyone.

Hangman didn't tell his children not to do this. He wanted them ready for anything.

Maeno seemed to have turned a corner, too. He still didn't go for his weapon or even seem to notice the creatures and noises around him, but he walked faster, kept up with the family better, and put more energy into the journey than before.

He held Mora's hand for most of the day, but he didn't ask her to carry him and he never slowed enough that she had to encourage him or prod him to keep up.

Hangman monitored all four of them on the march to see if any of them tired or needed to stop for a break. None of them said a word about it. None of the children complained even once.

The three children took food out of their bags and ate while they walked if they got hungry. They drank from any rivers or streams the family passed, but that was all.

The party didn't stop until nightfall. They made it as far as the base of the pass at the southern end of the valley. Hangman couldn't have been more pleased with their progress. This was better than he ever dared to hope.

The family camped in the trees again and everyone fell into a thoughtful silence. No one broke it, not even to talk about their studies.

The cohesion between the two adults and the three children had developed into something Hangman never would have expected, either. He'd never felt this with anyone but his male relatives and the men of his band on the journey north and then south.

He never thought he could feel anything like this for anyone but other men. He certainly never dreamed he could feel it for any women or children.

Mora and his children surpassed anything he had ever expected from any of them. They were far tougher than he gave them credit for. He trusted each of them with his life. He even trusted Maeno that way.

It wasn't Maeno's fault that he was only three. He was plenty tough enough for a three-year-old boy. He had to be if he survived that flood.

Now he was out here traveling with his older brother and sister and facing unknown dangers with a warrior's attitude. Any father would be proud of that.

Hangman could just imagine what champions his children would grow up into. He and Mora must have done something right to raise children like this.

Zaedi was only seven and Thena was only six—but they were as Godlessly brave, staunch, and tough as they would ever need to be. They would never be cowardly or weak. They would only rise and get stronger, braver, and more determined to conquer.

Hangman caught Mora making eye contact with him, but they didn't take it any further and they didn't talk.

They both seemed to have settled into a place beyond words where they already understood exactly what the other was thinking. He never thought he would ever trust her as much as he did now.

He pushed that thought out of his mind and the whole family bedded down for the night. No one spoke, not even when they woke up the next morning and did it all again.

A river flowed up between the two converging mountain ranges at the base of the pass. The family had no trouble following the river and hiking to the top. They stopped at the top of the pass and surveyed thousands upon thousands of miles of mountain country.

Mora pointed down the other side. "That's the nearest valley running north to south—and it does have jungle in it."

Hangman nodded. "Let's go."

That was the limit of their conversation. They made it to the bottom of the pass, found another river, and continued south from there.

The family fell into a set pattern of camping in the trees every night and traveling on the ground by day. The party climbed up into the branches and traveled through the canopy if any dangerous creatures came close enough to put the family in danger.

Hangman no longer saw anything wrong with avoiding these creatures. He didn't try to fight them. Fighting them would be foolhardy. He couldn't afford to take risks like that.

The family traveled until they ran out of food. Then Mora and the children stayed in the branches while Hangman hunted and processed the meat on the ground.

Mora and the children didn't come down to help him unless Mora wanted to brew another batch of Gooji juice for herself and him.

She continued to dose both of them for weeks after they left the valley. They both kept experiencing bouts of fever long after the wounds closed up. The wound sites kept getting hot and puffy even after the wounds themselves scarred over.

The fever and puffiness caused the most problems in Hangman's face. The fever sometimes spread to his brain. She gave him extra juice then. The symptoms didn't completely go away until three full months after she and Hangman received these bites.

The family traveled through countless valley systems. It took Hangman more than six months before he finally returned to the spot where he thought he had visited the band's east gorges camp as a child.

He obviously must have gotten confused because the camp wasn't there and neither was the band. It wasn't even the same gorge.

In the end, he and Mora had to backtrack all the way to the camp where Hammer's band had split from Shadow's band. Then Hangman could finally follow the route he knew to the eastern gorges.

The family didn't get there for an entire year. He finally strode through the gorges and entered the gorge where he knew for certain his father's band had camped before. Hangman remembered the spot well enough. This was definitely the same place.

Shadow's band wasn't here. "They could be wandering around in the mountains for decades," Hangman grumbled that night when they camped and built a fire in the empty gorge. "I might never see them again. They might all die out there."

"We could stay here," Mora suggested. "This gorge is well protected with only two ways in and out. We could do worse than staying here. They might show up in a few weeks or months."

"We should travel farther east and see if we can meet up with another Godless band."

She looked up. "There is another Godless band that we already know about."

He waved that away. "Maybe."

She left him alone for the rest of the evening and didn't intrude on his thoughts. He made up his mind in the dark that night not to join up with Hammer's band for a whole host of reasons.

Hangman didn't want to undermine Hammer's authority with his own people, but Hangman's decision went beyond that. Shadow would never forgive Hangman for joining up with Hammer.

Shadow might have been able to understand Hangman joining any other band if he couldn't find Shadow. Shadow would never be able to accept Hangman going over to Hammer, not even if they continued to treat each other as equals.

Shadow would consider that the ultimate betrayal. He would think that Hangman still supported Hammer's decision to leave. Hangman *did* still support that decision, but Hangman had always made every effort to avoid reminding Shadow of it.

Shadow wouldn't be able to ignore it if Hangman joined Hammer's band. Shadow would probably start to think that Hangman had left Shadow for the express purpose of joining another band.

Shadow might even accuse Hangman of cowardly running away from Shadow's authority. Hangman couldn't let that happen.

The next morning dawned as mornings always do. No one questioned him when he told his family that they had to travel east to meet up with another Godless band.

The family had to travel through dozens of different gorges. Jungle or at least vegetation grew and water flowed in streams on most of the gorge floors. The family had no problem traveling here.

They followed the same pattern of avoiding creatures whenever possible. Traveling this way turned out to be so much easier—and safer.

Chapter 25

T he family traveled for a week before they left the gorge country and came out into another jungle landscape. It stretched a long, long way eastward with no end in sight. Hangman couldn't see any other mountains over here.

The family climbed down into the jungle and traveled for most of the day. Hangman stopped in midafternoon when he heard human voices nearby.

He held up his hand to signal Mora and the children to stay where they were. He drew his kukris and crept through the undergrowth to see who it was. He was still deep inside Godless territory. He shouldn't encounter any enemy Clans here.

He crouched close to the ground and observed another Godless band sitting around a campfire. They hadn't built any shelters. They must be traveling, too.

He stood up, put his weapons away, and stepped out of the undergrowth so the other Godless could see him. All the men grabbed for their weapons, but they relaxed when they saw who it was.

Hangman raised both hands. "My name is Hangman, son of Shadow. I'm traveling through this country. Is this your territory?"

"We're traveling, too," one big man with tightly knotted hair told him. "We don't know if this country belongs to any particular band.

We're traveling east to meet up with another band we heard is living in a valley there."

Hangman studied everyone in the group. It consisted of nineteen men and eight women. They had five young children with them.

The same guy glanced behind Hangman's back. "Are you by yourself? It isn't safe to travel alone."

"I have my wife and children with me. I didn't bring them. I wanted to find out who it was first. We got separated from my father's band. We've been traveling alone for over a year trying to meet up with him and the rest of my family."

"You can travel with us if you want to." The guy stuck out his hand. "I'm Blaze."

Hangman shook his hand. "Are you Kral of this band?"

Blaze sat back down. "We don't really have a Kral—not anymore. We had one, but he died when another band attacked us. We haven't chosen another Kral since then. It didn't seem necessary when we have so few people. We're just traveling together. That's all."

"I understand." Hangman jerked his thumb over his shoulder. "I'll go get my wife and children. Traveling with another band will be better than traveling alone."

"You're all welcome," Blaze replied. "Any Godless are good enough for us."

Hangman returned to Mora and the children and brought them forward to meet up with the rest of the band. Blaze introduced his men one after another and the women introduced themselves to Mora. Then everyone sat down around the fire.

Blaze's people had cooked some fresh meat. They shared it with Hangman's family. The children of Blaze's group eyed Hangman's children, but they didn't mix.

"Where did you come from?" Blaze asked after a while.

"Our band was traveling through the gorge country northwest of here. Mora and the children got caught in a flood and I left the band to go look for them. We haven't seen our people since then. I returned to our original camp and retraced our steps to where I thought my father planned to take our band, but they weren't there. We came farther east to find another band to join up with."

Blaze arched his eyebrow and frowned. "Where was your original camp?"

Hangman described the location. Blaze listening. He only relaxed once he finally understood what Hangman meant. "That's all right, then," Blaze muttered.

"What's wrong?" Hangman asked. "Do you know Shadow's band?"

"It isn't that. The band that attacked us was Godless. Their Kral is Hammer. They attacked us unprovoked, killed most of our people, and carried off defenseless women and children."

Hangman raised his eyebrows. "Really? That sounds awful."

"They're the ones who killed our Kral. We were traveling along minding our own business and they came out of nowhere. They attacked again and again. They tracked us for miles and kept attacking to take out as many of our people as possible. They spared no one. This group right here—we barely got away with our lives."

Hangman turned to stare into the fire. He knew a lot of things—and he didn't know a lot of things.

He did know Hammer. There was absolutely no way on God's green Earth that Hammer's band attacked some other band of Godless unprovoked—and they definitely didn't carry off defenseless women and children. That simply did not happen.

Hangman sensed Mora sitting in silence across the circle. Neither she, Zaedi, nor Thena spoke up in Hammer's defense.

The story set off Hangman's alarm bells. So Blaze and his friends had a disastrous run-in with Hammer's band. Hammer and his men killed Blaze's Kral and a bunch of other people in their band.

It might have happened that way—all except the part about the attack being unprovoked.

Hangman could definitely picture Hammer doing something like that if he was provoked. Hangman could envision Hammer attacking ferociously if the other band provoked him enough.

The part about him carrying off defenseless women and children—that part might be true, too—except that this wouldn't have happened unprovoked, either.

Hammer and his men had grown up in captivity to the Renegade Clan. The Godless didn't carry off defenseless women and children—unless those women and children were already captives of someone else.

Hammer, his men, and their families had become extremely sensitive to this kind of thing. They simply would not stand by if they found out that Blaze and his party had been keeping women and children as captives.

Hammer's honor would have demanded that he intervene. His intervention wouldn't have gone well for the other band, especially once he found out that the other band was violating Godless law so badly.

Hangman didn't say any of that out loud. He didn't tell Blaze that he knew Hammer intimately and had raised him from boyhood to become the man who could actually pull off something like that. Blaze didn't need to know that—not now.

Mora turned away and went back to talking to the other women about their children. Hangman didn't pay attention to what they were talking about.

"How much do you know about the band you're trying to meet up with?" Hangman asked. "Do you know their Kral?"

"I don't know anything about them," Blaze replied. "I don't even know the man's name. I only heard they're camping at the junction where three rivers meet. We need to join with any band. We don't have enough people to defend ourselves. We don't care who we join up with as long as it isn't someone like Hammer. Anyone else is fine with us."

Hangman nodded. "We're in the same position. We would be grateful to travel with you."

Blaze shot a glance toward Mora and then the two older children. "You have a fine family."

"Do you have a family?" Hangman surveyed the group. "Are any of you married to these women?"

"Their husbands all died when Hammer's band attacked us. The women haven't paired off with anyone since. It's all too fresh for all of us. We just want to get somewhere safe before we think about any of that—and another Kral will probably want to decide who we go with or if he wants to give the women to his own men."

Hangman scrutinized the women a little more closely. None of them looked too broken up about their husbands' recent demise. These women looked absolutely petrified—mostly of him.

They held their children extra closely and stared at him with huge eyes. He couldn't figure out why—unless he was right about Blaze's party holding these women as captives. Was that even possible in a Godless band?

What provocation could possibly be worse than Blaze and his friends attacking Hammer's band and trying to carry off their women and underage girls? That would definitely be enough for Hammer to retaliate and try to wipe out an entire band.

It sounded like he had come pretty damn close to succeeding. The provocation must have been severe. Someone threatening Vina and the other girls the men had waited so long to marry—that would definitely have been enough to spark Hammer's fury.

Blaze and his friends didn't have a clue what they were messing with when they provoked Hammer. Blaze's band might have been going around marauding the countryside for years before they finally met their match—the idiots.

Hangman carried on a polite conversation with Blaze and the others for the rest of the evening. He made sure to sleep near Mora and the children that night.

Chapter 26

B laze and his party all got up the next morning and Mora and her family started traveling with them.

This band didn't make a habit of retreating into the canopy to avoid creatures or other dangers. The men stood their ground and fought any creature that threatened them.

The men worked together to bring down Crushers, Gorlocks, and even Stalkions who happened too close to the band. The band took advantage of these encounters to process the food for their journey. They didn't have to go hunting anywhere else.

The band only retreated into the canopy to avoid ants, Abnormits, and Krakelows. Hangman didn't argue with this and he didn't mention avoiding any other dangers. He went along with everything Blaze wanted to do.

Hangman didn't say anything about being Kral of his own band. He slipped right into being Blaze's subordinate. Hangman supported Blaze's decisions the same way Hangman had supported Shadow's decisions.

Hangman also didn't comment on Blaze's story about Hammer. No one mentioned Hammer again after that first night. Mora followed Hangman's example and kept silent about the connection between Hammer and their family.

The band traveled for a week and eventually came to a river. Blaze said it was one of the three that joined up with the others at the new band's location. The party started following the river.

The junction must have been farther away than Blaze realized. The band camped that night and Blaze gathered up his men to go scout the countryside ahead and find out if the band was nearby.

"We'll meet their Kral and negotiate if we can join them," he decided. "We'll get his decision before we bring the women and children up to meet him."

The men left. Mora settled into all the camp tasks she knew so well. She wound up working with three women named Rivila, Vosta, and Zona.

Rivila was older than the other two. Zona barely looked old enough to go to the gathering or maybe a year or two older than that.

"You have a beautiful daughter," Mora told Vosta while the two women collected water in their water skins—or Mora used water skins. The others used gourds.

Vosta looked away. "Thank you," she mumbled. "So do you."

"Did you only have the one child before your husband got killed?" Mora glanced behind her. "I'm surprised your band doesn't have more children. They usually run into the jungle for safety when someone attacks."

Vosta didn't answer at all and Rivila joined them just then. Mora smiled at her. These women acted strangely. They didn't act either friendly or hostile. They acted scared. Rivila hadn't said a single word to Mora since she joined this band.

"I'm sorry to hear about your husbands," she went on. "That must have been terrible. I wouldn't want to go through an attack like that—but I suppose it would have been worse for the women that Hammer's band carried off."

"No one carried them off!" Rivila blurted out.

Mora spun around. "They didn't?"

"Of course not! Those women left of their own free will." Rivila grimaced. "I wish now that I had gone with them, but I was too scared of Lifeless."

Mora stared at the women with huge eyes. "What happened?"

Rivila made another face. "Lifeless's band went around the countryside raiding other Godless and stealing women and supplies. I don't even know if the original band *was* Godless. They could have come from any Clan and posed as Godless so unsuspecting bands would take them in. Lifeless tried to do the same thing to Hammer, but he didn't buy it. He saw through Lifeless's fake kindness and expelled Lifeless's band from his territory."

Mora gulped. "Wow."

"Lifeless didn't listen. They armed for war, but Hammer was ready and defeated them easily. Lifeless had to hide the women and children before the assault and a bunch of captive women from Lifeless's band used the battle as a chance to run away and go to Hammer. He took them in. I suppose they're still living there."

Mora tried to look away. "That sounds incredible."

Rivila chopped her hand through the air. "We're all captives. Don't you get that? Hammer never killed our husbands. Lifeless did. Now Blaze plans to do the same thing to this new band as soon as we find them. He'll do the same thing to you. You better be careful or he'll kill your husband and your sons and keep you and your daughter as prisoners. Why do you think we only have daughters?"

Mora frowned. "But....you have two boys with you."

"They're Shark's and Ruin's sons," Rivila snapped. "Both men took captive women for themselves and fathered those boys. Those are the only boys Blaze and his men keep around—their own sons. They kill any others—or if the women give birth to any sons."

Mora bent over the water in front of her. "Thank you for telling me."

"If you're smart, you'll tell your husband to get you out of here tonight," Rivila went on. "You'll get as far away from these rotten bastards as you can. Your family is better off traveling alone."

Rivila shot to her feet and left all her gourds lying there on the ground where she had dropped them. She stormed off and seemed to forget all about getting water.

Vosta wouldn't look at Mora. Vosta picked up her gourds and went back to the camp. The two women left Mora with plenty on her mind.

She had already realized the minute Blaze started talking about Hammer that Blaze must have been lying. He had either highly colored the tale or he just made it up—probably to cover up the fact that Lifeless's party was the one that attacked unprovoked.

Mora never believed for an instant that Hammer's band had carried off another band's women. Hammer and his men had left their families and risked everything for a handful of girls they loved. The men had no interest in another band's women.

Mora went back to the camp in a little while and busied herself with her children. She stayed in the camp, but she didn't make it too obvious that she was keeping her children near her.

She took them out for a walk in the jungle by themselves so she could give them another reading and writing lesson without arousing anyone's suspicions.

She returned a few hours later just as Blaze, Hangman, and the others returned. Hangman sat down near Mora and the children. He was the only man here who acted at all affectionate or protective of any woman or her children.

Mora had already detected something seriously wrong in this band. Now she saw it all as plain as day. None of these people were couples—not in the traditional Godless sense.

The men kept their distance from the women the way real Godless men would have kept their distance from women they weren't legally married to. The two sides didn't mix.

Blaze talked to his men across the camp. He mentioned that he didn't find the other band, but he had picked up their trail heading down the river toward the river junction. He assured everyone that they would catch up with the new band in the next few days.

Mora glanced over at Hangman. Was this new band Shadow's band? He met her gaze. His communicated so much.

The men had killed a Dushag while they were out. The women started cooking it to prepare the evening meal. Mora helped them for a while and then Hangman left to go down to the river by himself.

Mora waited what she hoped would be an appropriate amount of time, told Zaedi to keep an eye on his brother and sister, and raced after Hangman to catch up with him.

She found him squatted by the water's edge. He watched another Dushag arch through the current while he cupped the water into his mouth.

She squatted down next to him. "Those women....they're all captives," she blurted out. "They told me Blaze and the others plan to kill you and the boys. Then the band will take me and Thena as captives. They've been marauding the countryside for years. The women say the band tried to do the same thing to Hammer's band, but he retaliated."

"I know," Hangman murmured.

"You know?!" she countered. "We have to get out of here! We have to get as far away from them as possible."

"No, we'll stay with them," he replied. "This band ahead of us could be Shadow's band—and even if they aren't, I have to warn them so they know what's coming. The best way to stop these people is to stay near them. We'll be able to defeat them when the time comes. Then we can free the women and girls. We wouldn't be able to do that if we left now."

She slumped. "Do we have to?"

He smiled at her. "I know you better than that. Don't tell me you would leave captive women and girls with these traitorous vipers. We've come too far for that."

Mora groaned and covered her eyes. "We've been traveling all this time and we had to meet up with the one Godless band that does this. Rivila says she isn't even sure they are Godless. She thinks they could be some other Clan posing as Godless."

"I wouldn't be surprised. The good news is that they'll lead us straight to another band that *is* Godless—real Godless. We'll wait until Blaze gets ready to strike. Then we'll break away, warn the other band, and help them defeat Blaze. Then the other band will take us in."

"I sure hope you're right."

"I don't want to travel alone anymore and I know you don't, either. Blaze and his men can give us protection in the meantime until we meet up with another band. We might get lucky and this other band will be Shadow's band. That would be best." He leaned over and kissed her on the forehead. "Come on. Let's get back. I don't want to leave the children alone."

Mora followed him back to camp and they both sat down near their children. Rivila went from one person to the next handing out the Dushag meat she'd already cooked.

Rivila always went around everywhere with a permanent scowl plastered across her face. Now Mora knew why.

Hangman, Mora, and the children thanked her and ate in silence. Mora saw more than she ever wanted to see of the dynamic between Blaze's men and their captive women. One big man named Fence got hold of Zona.

Fence didn't comb, braid, arrange, decorate, or even wash his hair. It grew in one matted plate of solid, tangled filth down his back. He never did anything with it. He never even touched it.

He towered over Zona and grabbed her arm hard enough to make her cry out. He leaned all the way toward her and snarled in her face while she cowered away from him and leaned all the way over backward as far as her bound arm would let her go.

He asked her something and she shrieked out, "NO!!" way too loudly before he clubbed her to the ground with his fist.

She sprawled in the dirt sobbing her eyes out. He didn't wait for her to get up by herself. He grabbed her arm again, dragged her to her feet, and marched her away into the jungle where no one could see them.

Now Mora knew with absolutely no doubt that Blaze, Lifeless, and their men never had been Godless. The Godless didn't act violently toward women and children. They didn't believe in acting violently toward anyone but their enemies and traitors to the Clan.

The other men, women, and children pretended not to see the altercation between Fence and Zona. Everyone went on eating as though it never happened.

Fence and Zona came back an hour later. He sat down with the other men and she went back to work. She kept crying for a long time afterward. She refused to look at or talk to anyone. None of the women showed her an ounce of comfort or said a word to encourage her.

Mora got busy bedding down her children. At least Hangman stayed close to them every night. He never slept anywhere else.

She sure hoped he was right about this plan. This band was the absolute last place Mora wanted to be right now—and it was the last place she wanted him and her children to be right now, too.

Chapter 27

Hangman woke up the next morning when he heard Maeno laughing. Hangman sat up and squinted at Mora playing some kind of game with him with the colored stones from his bag.

Zaedi and Thena stood aside watching with their usual serious expressions. No one had to draw them a picture of what was going on in this band.

Hangman got to his feet, ate some of the Dushag meat left over from last night, and went down to the river to wash his face. He didn't stay long. He didn't want to leave Mora and the children alone with Blaze and the others on the march.

Hangman returned and helped her pack up their belongings and organize the children to move out. Zaedi and Thena were already ready to go. Maeno accepted it without any fuss when Mora told him to put his stones away and pick up his bags.

They all stood up and set off down the river again. Blaze and his men hadn't found the other band's tracks until late in the afternoon yesterday. Blaze's band didn't find the trail again until the same time today, so of course they didn't catch up with the other band.

Blaze called a halt at sunset and everyone made camp. The women went about their business, refilled all their empty water gourds, and shared out the dried food from the band's previous kills.

A few different men scouted the terrain ahead, but they didn't stay out long. They came back soon enough and a different man named Ruin started slapping Rivila around.

Hangman watched from a distance. Ruin didn't seem too interested in taking Rivila off anywhere by themselves or even taking advantage of her here in front of everyone.

He just slapped her a few times, punched her in the stomach, and then belted her hard enough to knock her out. No one went over to help her. No one even checked to see if she was okay.

Mora came back in a little while and sat down with Hangman and their children. She didn't look sideways at Rivila, either. That was odd. Mora had made it sound like she and Rivila were on speaking terms. Rivila had been the one to confide in Mora.

It definitely wasn't like Mora to just ignore someone in trouble. Blood trickled out of Rivila's nose. Mora must have been able to see that. She smiled at Hangman when he studied her. Then she went straight back to repairing a hole in one of her water bags.

Rivila didn't come around until long past dark. She groaned, rolled over, and sat up with her hair scattered all over her face. She looked around and her usual scowl spread across her features when she surveyed the camp.

She outright glared at Ruin, but he didn't notice. He was too busy talking to Blaze and the others.

Just then, Blaze stood up and said, "We'll see," to his men. He started to turn away to walk across the camp. His gaze swept the area. "Where's Fence?" he snapped over his shoulder.

"Who knows?" a man named Rust replied.

Blaze strode across the camp yelling out, "Fence! Get over here!"

No one answered him. No one paid attention at first.

Blaze shrugged it off and went back to sit with his men. They went on with their discussion until darkness settled over the camp.

Blaze stalked over to Zona. "Where's Fence? Did he tell you where he was going?"

She stared up at him with huge, terrified eyes and shook her head. He went back to his men. "Which of you has seen Fence?"

"He said he was going out hunting," a man named Coal replied. "That was right after we got here."

Blaze frowned. "That isn't like him."

No one else paid much attention and the discussion shifted. Fence still had not returned by the time everyone went to sleep.

He wasn't in camp by the time everyone woke up the next morning. Blaze delayed the band's departure. He kept expecting Fence to turn up, but in the end, Blaze shrugged that off, suggested that Fence would catch up, and the band moved out.

The party followed their quarry's footprints along the river. Blaze called two stops that day. Hangman watched Mora being extra nice to Zona and Rivila.

Mora paid a lot of attention to two other women, both of whom walked around with bruises all over their faces and bodies. One was another young girl named Ruda. The other woman was named Chida and she was much older than everyone else.

Hangman didn't see how these women had gotten their bruises. Two of the men made a point of taking these women out into the jungle alone and bringing them back more banged up than they already were.

Ruda belonged to a man named Shark. He was a huge guy who kept his long braids tied close to his scalp. They combined into something like a crown that ringed his head in a tube of black.

Chida belonged to a man named Host. Whoever had initiated these men obviously preferred short, one-syllable names.

The other possibility was that whoever instructed these people to impersonate the Godless must have chosen these names at random to make them sound Godless.

Zona relaxed considerably around Mora that day, now that Zona didn't have to worry about Fence bothering her.

Hangman had developed an instant dislike of the man. Fence didn't keep himself clean and he stank. Hangman didn't like being anywhere he might smell Fence—which was anywhere within a hundred yards of the guy.

Fence's comrades didn't seem to notice the smell. They didn't seem to notice anything out of the ordinary about Fence's total lack of hygiene, especially when it came to his hair. No true Godless man would ever have worn his hair like that.

Real Godless men took pride in keeping their hair neat. Alien had spent hours every week taking apart all the knots on his head, brushing out his hair, washing it meticulously, and then winding it all back up into knots.

Cheina had done this job for him during their married years together, but he had taken exceptional care of his hair all his life before that. Shadow had even told the story that Alien started to wear his hair like that when he was still an uninitiated boy.

Alien didn't give a damn if anyone teased him about it. He was proud of the way it made him look and he took pride in the effort he put into maintaining it. All Godless men did. No red-blooded Godless man would have gotten caught dead with his hair out of place.

Fence still had not returned that evening when the band made camp. Blaze paced around searching everywhere. Coal and Rust wanted to backtrack along their route and look for Fence, but Blaze told them not to.

Fence still had not returned by the end of the second day. "It isn't like him to just vanish," Blaze muttered.

Coal and Rust made the same suggestion again and Blaze agreed.

"Go back to the spot where we lost him," Blaze ordered. "Track him out of camp and find the son of a bitch, dead or alive. We'll wait for you to come back and tell us what's going on."

Everyone else settled down to wait. Blaze sent Ruin and Host to follow the new band's tracks, catch up with them, and announce Blaze's intentions to the new band's Kral.

The two men left. Mora didn't sit with Hangman and the children that night. She stayed with Zona and the other women. They worked together for a while and then went down to the river for water.

She came back to get her water skins before she left. "Are you going to be all right while I'm gone?" she asked Hangman.

"Sure. We aren't going anywhere for a while."

She kissed him and left with her new friends. They didn't come back until close to sundown.

When they did, Rivila carried Mora's water skins and Mora carried another Dushag she had killed by the river. She laughed with the other women. They all acted so much lighter with her around.

Their attitude rankled Blaze and the other men. They glared at Mora and the women when the women squatted down by Chida's fire and started cutting up the Dushag.

Hangman didn't stop Thena from going over there to help out—and then Maeno went over there to sit next to Mora. She kissed him on the head and went right on talking to the other women.

Hangman and Zaedi stayed where they were. "Mother looks much happier," Zaedi remarked.

Hangman nodded. She did look happy. He tried to remember when he'd seen her this happy. The last time was when they lived in the northern valley—before Alien's death. Had it really been that long since he'd seen her laughing and talking to other women like this?

He didn't understand how she could act like this when these women were living as brutalized captives with a bunch of marauders. She was the one who said she didn't want to stay here.

Her attitude infected the other women. They acted a lot more relaxed, talked more freely, and laughed more often. Even Zona laughed and talked back and forth with Mora.

Hangman put the matter aside, but it all came to a head when the band woke up that morning and Coal and Rust returned.

"We couldn't find him," Rust reported to Blaze.

"What do you mean—you couldn't find him?!" Blaze fired back. "You must have found something. You must have found some sign of a struggle or a creature attack."

Coal shook his head. "His footprints just vanished without a trace. He was walking through the jungle one minute and his footsteps evaporated the next—and he vanished somewhere he wouldn't have been able to get into the trees. He's just...gone."

"That's impossible!" Blaze snapped. "A man can't just disappear into thin air!"

Rust shrugged. "We're just telling us what we saw. We found his tracks clear enough. He left the camp and was walking through soft soil. There's no mistake. It was him."

"Then where the hell is he?!" Blaze roared.

The two men couldn't tell him anything. The news unsettled everyone—everyone except the women. They didn't laugh and talk this morning, but they walked around with a lighter step than usual.

Blaze paced and scowled at everything. He spoke in short, clipped responses when anyone spoke to him. He kept telling everyone that the band would leave as soon as Host and Ruin came back.

They didn't come back all day. It shouldn't have taken them that long to catch up with the other band. The men should have come straight back even if the other Kral agreed to accept Blaze's party.

Blaze practically bellowed at everyone the next morning when he woke up and discovered that Ruin and Host still hadn't returned.

He roared at Rust and Coal to go out and find the two men. Rust and Coal were the band's best trackers.

A thick cloud of tension hung over the other men until Rust and Coal returned at sunset and reported that they'd found exactly the same thing. Host and Ruin had both vanished without a trace.

Rivila actually burst out laughing when she heard the news. "Ha ha!" she gloated. "That rotten son of a bitch got what he deserved at last! He'll never lay another finger on me!"

"Shut your mouth, old woman!" Blaze snapped. "No one needs you around."

She only leered at him. "Do you think you can do anything to me worse than what he's already done? All of you bastards will get exactly what you deserve! Host and Fence were only the first. You'll all die and the world will be better off without you."

She laughed at Blaze again and went back to the other women. People like Chida openly congratulated her. Zona stayed near Chida and Rivila that night, too.

Blaze ordered everyone to move out the next day. They had already lost too much time on this—and now the band only had sixteen men to protect everyone. The band couldn't afford to lose anyone else.

Chapter 28

Mora put her water skins on the ground next to Zaedi and Thena, squatted down next to one of the cooking fires, and started helping Zona skin a dead Demonex the men had killed that day.

Blaze didn't want to stop yet, but the band had been getting low on food. He had to give the women time to process and dry all the meat for the rest of the journey.

He kept pacing around glaring at everyone. Another man named Bitter had disappeared on the march in the middle of the day. He had been walking right next to the band before he vanished without a trace.

No one had noticed his disappearance until the band stopped for the evening. That was the strangest part. None of the party could remember anything happening to him. One minute he was there. The next he was gone.

Mora looked up from her work when Hangman reentered the camp. She had been keeping a close eye on him all day. He hadn't been anywhere near Bitter—and he hadn't left the camp for long enough to have killed Fence, Host, or Ruin.

No one could figure out how or why these men kept disappearing without anyone knowing what was going on. Blaze and his men stood over there on the other side of the camp right now and talked with their heads together.

The women didn't talk or laugh the way they did before, but the atmosphere among them had lightened considerably since the men had started disappearing.

Bitter didn't have a woman of his own, but he had been known to be cruel and unforgiving to all the women and children.

None of the women and girls acted too upset or grief-stricken over the loss of these men. Rivila had been the only woman to outright laugh about it.

Zona kept quiet about Fence and kept her head down, but she didn't act as scared. None of the women acted scared anymore.

Mora tried to read Hangman's expression on his way toward her and the children. He'd been acting much more thoughtful these last few days. He seemed to take the mystery much more seriously than the other men did.

The men just acted worried—and maybe even scared for their lives. Hangman didn't act scared. That set him apart from the others. He was the only man in the band who didn't act like he was walking around with a target on his forehead.

His arrival caused an instant reaction among the other men. Blaze spun around and pointed at Hangman. "You! You did it! You're the one who killed them."

Hangman raised his eyebrows. "How could I do that when I've been right here in camp with you the whole time?"

"You haven't been here the *whole* time!" Blaze snapped. "You just left right now! You could have done something."

"Something like what? All the rest of you have been here. I just went down to the river to get a drink of water. It isn't like I killed someone while I was away—and I was nowhere near Bitter today. You all saw me. I was at the head of the line and he was in the back. I was in camp in sight of all of you when Host and Ruin left. I couldn't have followed them and I was in camp when Fence went missing. When do you say I could have done anything?"

Blaze didn't listen. He sliced his finger at his men. "Tie him up. We traveled for years without a single incident before he came along."

The men surrounded Hangman. Mora shot to her feet and rushed over there. "Hey! You can't do this! Leave him alone!"

Shark straight-armed her away. The men wrestled Hangman to the ground, disarmed him, and started to tie him up.

"You're making a mistake," he called up to Blaze. "I'm not the one killing your men. They'll keep disappearing. I'm telling you the truth."

"You're the only one around here that we can't trust. Put him over there."

Zaedi came over. Mora pulled him toward her to stop him from intervening. The men dragged Hangman bound hand and foot to a tree at the edge of camp.

The women stood off to one side watching. None of them intervened, either. The men sat Hangman on the ground and wound lengths of rope around his chest to bind him to the tree. Then Shark, Rust, and a man named Acid stood guard over him as night fell.

Hangman made eye contact with Mora across the camp. He still didn't look scared. His gaze unnerved her, so she took Zaedi back to their side of the camp. The other women were already finishing the Demonex. She didn't rejoin them.

She talked to her children instead. They had developed a different spoken form of their spelling game that they could play without actually writing anything down. They could play in full view of everyone else in camp as long as the children kept their voices low.

She murmured more difficult words to them and they tried to spell them. Then she told them whole sentences and they recited them back by spelling out each word one letter at a time. They were starting to work on improving their punctuation.

Then Maeno said he wanted to play, so Zaedi and Thena gave him much simpler words he could actually spell.

They had to stop talking when Rivila came over and delivered some of the Demonex meat to Mora and the children. Rivila gave them more than their share. Mora removed some from each bowl, added it to a fifth bowl, and took it across the camp to Hangman.

Shark tried to stop her. "No one is allowed near the prisoner."

"Aren't you at least going to feed him?" Mora asked. "Blaze never said he had to starve while he was tied up. You can give it to him yourself if you don't trust me to go near him."

She held out the bowl. Shark slapped it out of her hand, sent the food spilling into the dirt, and then backhanded her hard enough to bring the taste of blood into her mouth.

She stumbled away and returned to her children. She didn't look at anyone else all night. She couldn't look at Hangman. Shark had hit her right in front of her husband.

That would have been a crime punishable by death in any real God-less band. The husband would have been entitled to kill the attacker on the spot for such an insult.

Hangman just sat there watching in silence. He didn't move. He didn't respond when Shark said something over his shoulder and kicked both the food and the bowl away.

He got them both much dirtier and made the food inedible. No one went near Hangman again for the rest of the night.

Mora sat up and rubbed her aching cheek the next morning. Hangman leaned in the same place tied up against the tree. He watched everything with his usual calm, alert gaze. Did he sleep at all last night? Did he see someone sneak out to kill one of the men?

Three different men named Hook, Giddy, and Screech stood guard over him. Shark, Acid, and Rust were gone. Rust lay sprawled on the ground not far away. Mora didn't see Shark or Acid.

Blaze was just waking up. He glared at Hangman. Blaze stormed through the camp barking orders at everyone to get up and get moving. He ordered Hook, Giddy, and Screech to untie Hangman but to keep his wrists bound.

The band got ready to leave only for Blaze to discover Acid gone. Blaze went on a rampage demanding to know where Acid was, but no amount of searching would uncover his whereabouts.

"Now do you believe me?" Hangman interrupted. "Your men have been standing guard over me all night. I couldn't have done anything."

Blaze ignored him except to order Hook, Giddy, and Screech to keep a hold on Hangman all day if necessary.

They did. They marched him bound at the wrists at the front of the line when the band moved out. "We should do something to help your husband," Chida murmured to Mora on the way. "He's such a kind man."

Mora snorted. "You don't have to worry about him. He can take care of himself. Blaze's men are in the most danger here."

Ruda overheard them and cast a hasty glance around at the other men. "Which one of them could be doing it? Someone in this party is a killer. We could be next."

"Do you ever notice that it's the cruelest men who die first?" Chida pointed out. "I think one of you is doing it."

"Us?! Rivila countered. "*We* couldn't be doing it!"

"Why not?" Mora asked. "You all have a reason to hate these men."

"None of us could have attacked these men without leaving some sign of a scuffle," Rivila pointed out. "None of us can fight well enough to kill one of these men. We definitely don't know enough to make them vanish without a trace."

The women had to stop talking just then when Blaze came down the line studying everyone. He paid special attention to the men, but they were all still accounted for—all the men who had been alive at the beginning of the day.

They kept walking for the rest of the day. Blaze stopped more than once and kept wondering aloud how much farther away the other band was. He thought the party should have caught up by now, but the constant problems and delays had slowed everyone down.

He admitted to his men that he wanted to send some of them ahead to at least warn the other Kral that this new band was approaching and that their intentions were purely honorable—which they obviously weren't.

Then again, maybe Blaze was starting to rethink his strategy. Maybe he wanted to go under another Kral to save himself from whoever might be threatening this band now.

Blaze didn't dare to send anyone ahead—not after what happened to Host and Ruin. Blaze kept everyone together no matter what.

He would have kept marching much later, but the party had to stop again when they came face to face with another pack of Demonex. A lot of them seemed to live in this country.

They turned on the band as soon as the first men walked into view. The Demonex spread out and loped a few paces closer to the band.

"Let me go," Hangman urged Blaze. "You know I'm not the one killing your men. Give me my weapons back. You don't have enough men to defend the band as it is."

Blaze compressed his lips, took one more look at the Demonex, and ordered his men to free Hangman and give him his kukris. Mora hung back with the women and children.

The Demonex stopped advancing when they saw so many armed men getting ready to fight them. The Demonex eventually paced sideways and left so the band could continue on its way.

Chapter 29

H angman sat down next to Mora and the children. She didn't wait for him to ask before she put a bowl of cooked meat into his hands.

"I'm sorry about last night," she mumbled.

He glanced at the bruise on her face. "That won't go unpunished. I swear it."

She looked away. "You're in enough trouble already, aren't you?"

"Not at all. I'm the only man here that everyone knows isn't the killer. They can suspect each other until doomsday. That's one good thing about last night. No one suspects me anymore. I can't be the killer."

She looked up at him with those deep eyes of hers. "Do you have an idea who it might be?"

He shrugged. "I can think of a lot of people who wanted those men dead. We'll see. I'm sure it will come to light soon. The band won't be able to go on with so few men if this keeps up."

"What will happen then?"

"At least Shadow or whoever the other Kral is won't have to worry about these men. Something tells me the women and girls don't plan to ambush the other band."

She put a piece of food into her mouth and ate in silence. The bruise on the side of her face infuriated him, but he didn't mention it again.

He would get his own back if it was the last thing he ever did. No one would lay a hand on his wife right in front of him and live to tell the tale.

Shark already had lived to tell the tale. He was still walking around free over there on the other side of the camp and giving Ruda a hard time about going out into the jungle with him later. She burst into tears when he told her.

She actually fell on her knees and begged him not to, but he only slapped her and told her to shut up.

Hangman probably would have started plotting these men's demise if the killer hadn't already been doing it for him. The question was how the killer was doing it without leaving any trace of attack or even leaving a body behind. Hangman didn't understand it.

None of the women could have done it. Mora was probably the most skilled fighter here, but not even she could have killed Fence or Acid—not without getting injured or at least leaving some track or sign.

Hangman had seen plenty of Coal's and Rust's tracking skills in action. If they said the killer left no trace, then the killer really must have done their work. Hangman himself couldn't have done that much.

He had killed plenty of his enemies in his time, but he always left some trace. He didn't try to hide it. He wasn't sure he even knew how.

The party made camp that night. Hangman slept with his arms around Mora all night long. Then the camp went into another uproar the next morning when everyone discovered Giddy gone.

Blaze ordered three of the men to stand guard while the remaining seven went to search for Giddy. Hangman was one of the seven who went to search. Everyone spread outward and entered the jungle to look for Giddy.

Coal and Rust followed his tracks, but Blaze told the others to cover all the rest of the surrounding terrain in case Coal and Rust missed anything.

Hangman's path led northward away from the river. He searched the ground for any footprints. He didn't see anything, but he didn't expect to. None of the band had come this way.

They had only just camped on this spot last night. No one in the band had any reason to come this way. The women had been going back and forth between the camp and the river. No one had needed to go hunting. The band already had enough food.

Hangman walked for half an hour before he gave it up. Giddy wouldn't be over here. He had no reason to come here. He had been alive and well last night when Hangman went to sleep. The killer must have struck in the middle of the night.

Hangman headed south from his current position. He planned to circle back behind Coal and Rust and hopefully pick up Giddy's tracks somewhere over there.

Hangman could conceivably believe that Giddy might have re-traced the band's route back in the direction from which the party had come. Maybe Giddy thought he could find Acid there. Who knew?

Hangman didn't know anyone in the band with any particular grudge against Giddy—not the way Zona, Rivila, and Chida held grudges against Fence, Ruin, and Host.

Giddy must have helped abduct these women in the first place, though. The women and their families could have all kinds of history with Giddy that Hangman didn't know about. He really knew noth-ing about these people and didn't want to.

What if the killer came after him next—or Mora and the children? Something told him that wouldn't happen. Rivila had laughed at Blaze when he found out that Ruin was gone. Hangman just couldn't get that out of his head. She had celebrated Ruin's death.

The killer had a beef against these men. The killer had no reason to kill Hangman. He could think of a few people who did have a reason to kill him, but it wouldn't be anyone in this band.

He made it a hundred yards, curved farther southeast, and stopped in his tracks when he heard a loud twang coming from the trees ahead. He knew that sound. It wasn't the sound of any jungle creature.

He froze to the spot and looked around everywhere. Movement told him where to look.

He stared up into the canopy at Shark whistling past him into the high branches. A rope lashed around his broken neck and yanked him off the ground with a vicious crack when a young sapling snapped back into place. Someone had bent it over and tied it down.

The sapling swayed for a minute. Its motion made Shark swing at the end of his rope. His arms, legs, and head hung limp from his lifeless body.

Hangman stared up at the guy as all the puzzle pieces clicked into place. Hangman had heard that twanging sound only one other place. He had heard it when the Anglers set off his snares and boobytraps in the valley.

That's how the killer must be getting rid of these men. That's how the killer removed them from the scene of the crime without a trace—by yanking them off the ground with incredible force—enough force to kill them instantly and leave not one hint of a struggle.

Hangman could think of only one person around here who knew enough to pull off a trap like that—someone other than himself. He didn't have to wonder anymore.

The sapling bowed its crown down to the ground pointing the other way—away from the place Shark had been coming from.

Hangman advanced through the trees and saw Mora crouching in the branches at a distance from the sapling. She sat in the crook of a tree trunk fifteen feet off the ground. That's how she hid her movements—by traveling through the branches.

Blaze's party wasn't Godless. Hangman had never seen them travel in the branches even once. They only climbed high enough to get away from ants and Abnormits.

The men didn't teach their women and children to climb. The band always slept on the ground no matter what—and they always lit fires.

Coal and Rust probably didn't know enough of Godless ways even to look for the signs that someone had been hiding, moving, or climbing into the branches. It probably never crossed their minds that the killer might have struck from the canopy.

Mora pulled on a second rope attached to the sapling's crown. She had to use all her weight to bend it over until she lowered Shark's body to the ground.

She lowered him into an ant's nest. The ants enveloped him, devoured his body until not even a drop of blood remained, and then gnawed the bones to nothing, too.

She returned the sapling to its former position the minute the ants chewed through the rope around his neck. She didn't just let the sapling go. She uncoiled the rope hand over hand until it straightened up.

She left the rope hanging there, scrambled into the branches, and took off at high speed heading back to camp.

Chapter 30

H angman met up with Blaze, Coal, and Rust. Hangman reported in all truthfulness that he hadn't seen any trace of Giddy anywhere. Now Hangman knew why. No one would ever find Giddy—or any of the others.

The men returned to camp in a furor when they realized that Shark was gone, too. Blaze stormed through the camp raging at everyone that a man couldn't just vanish off the face of the Earth without even leaving a track.

Hangman sat in silence through the whole tirade. A man most definitely could vanish off the face of the earth without leaving a single track. Mora had proven that.

Hangman didn't look at her beyond the usual eye contact. He didn't say anything to her about seeing her kill Shark. She must have killed all the others the same way.

That must be how she was doing all of this without anyone noticing her gone. She must have been laying traps for these men, killing them, and leaving their bodies to the ants to erase all the evidence of her actions.

He had been holding her in his arms all night last night. She couldn't have left without waking him up. Now he knew how she did it. She must have laid the snare earlier in the afternoon—probably when she went to get water.

She always went to get water, but she always went with other women. She could have given them some excuse to separate from them at least for a little while. Then she could rejoin them and make it back into camp long before her next victim left to meet his fate.

That was the thing about these traps. The victim could spring the trap long after she laid it. She didn't have to be anywhere nearby to kill these men.

Hangman spent most of the evening thinking about how to deal with this. He would have had to say something about it if he had been Kral of this band—or her Kral. He *was* her Kral, but he couldn't bring himself to say anything.

She was a Follower to her core. This was her ruthless way of killing her enemies. She didn't want to wait for them to attack her or her family or the other band or anyone else—so she killed these men first.

She killed with more frightening merciless cunning than anyone Hangman had ever met. She showed no pity. She didn't give these men the chance to fight back. She broke their necks instantaneously. They never found out who killed them.

The women listened in silence while Blaze went into hysterics over Shark's disappearance. Blaze got in Ruda's face and straight up accused her of killing Shark when she had been inside the camp and under guard the whole time.

Mora had not been inside the camp and under guard the whole time. How did she get away from the guards? None of the three men in question offered any explanation.

None of the women piped up to inform Blaze that Mora had suddenly gone missing for however long it took her to go out to the jungle, lower Shark's body into the ant nest, and then get back to the camp before anyone noticed her missing.

Was it possible that the women already knew that Mora was the killer? Were they covering for her so she could continue to carry out this invisible reign of terror on their archenemies?

She definitely didn't hit Shark from a distance that time. She had been right there on hand the minute her trap snatched him off the ground. Did she go out to the jungle and set the trap right before he walked into it?

Hangman could picture Acid falling into one of her traps while she had been asleep in her husband's arms in the camp. She hadn't been there for that—and Coal and Rust didn't find Acid swinging from a rope around his neck. How did she get him into the ant's nest?

Hangman couldn't figure any of this out no matter how much he thought about it. He had to do something about this—but what?

He was still thinking about it the next morning when the band headed east along the river again. He kept his eye on her all day. She never left the company of the other women. He never let her out of his sight, but she still managed to kill Screech on the way.

Blaze didn't say a word this time when the band finally camped. The women worked in silence while the remaining men whispered to each other at a distance. They didn't invite Hangman to join them.

He accompanied Mora to the river with Ruda and Chida. She only smiled at him. She looked so innocent.

She also looked Godless. These men didn't know the Followers' ways. They didn't know enough to recognize when someone was using Follower methods against them. They probably didn't know they were at war against one woman half their size.

She laughed and talked with the other women. She finished filling her water skins first and joked with them that her husband must be hanging around because he wanted her to go back to the camp instead of shooting the breeze with them.

He didn't say anything to contradict this. He walked back to the camp with her.

"I know, Mora," he told her on the way.

She looked up at him and frowned. "Excuse me?"

"I know what you're doing. I saw you kill Shark. I know you're the one killing these men."

She stopped in her tracks and faced him. She showed not one shred of remorse. "So what if I am?" she demanded. "What difference does it make if I do? They're scumbags. They're worse than Renegades and Bounty Hunters. At least Renegades and Bounty Hunters have their Clan laws to justify their actions. These assholes are passing themselves off as Godless and making the Godless look bad. They all deserve to die for what they've done. I don't care if I kill every last one of them—and that's what I'll do. I won't wait around for them to attack the other band—which need I remind you might be Shadow's band? These men are a danger to everyone, including us—especially us. I won't stop until I kill them all."

He took a few steps closer and lowered his voice. "I'm not here to tell you to stop. I'm proud of you for what you're doing."

Her eyes popped. "You are?!"

"Of course. It's ingenious. I don't want you to stop. There are only ten men left. Kill a few more of them. Then you and I will carry out a surprise attack to kill all the rest. None of the others are strong enough to resist the two of us working together. We'll wipe them all out and take the women and children to the new band."

She blinked at him in disbelief. "Really?"

"Really. I can help you, now that I know what you're doing. I can buy you some extra time to sneak out of camp—but you don't even really need my help. Just do what you're already doing. Just don't get caught. Okay?"

"Um...." She gulped. "Okay. I can do that."

He smiled at her reaction. He kissed her, but she was too stunned to respond. "I'm proud of you. Not even I could figure out how you were doing it until I saw you with my own eyes. I'm quite sure the other men can't figure it out, either. They must be shaking in their shoes wondering who will be next."

She swallowed hard. "Uh...okay. I guess....we better get back."

He accompanied her back to camp. The men didn't notice Hangman and Mora return. They probably never paid enough attention to the women to notice if any of them came or went. The women were beneath the men's notice.

Mora sat with Hangman and the children for a while. Then she went to help the other women. Thena went with her.

Hangman watched them from a distance. He could not have picked a better example for his daughter to follow. Mora would teach Thena to grow up to be a proud, ferocious, deadly Godless woman. Thena would never hesitate to defend her family and her band.

Zaedi broke in on Hangman's thoughts. "Is something bothering you, Father?"

Hangman turned around. "Hmm? No, not at all. Why do you ask that, my son?"

"You were just frowning like something was bothering you."

Hangman shook that off and forced himself to turn his back on Mora. "I was just thinking about this killer who keeps making the men disappear."

"Are you sure it's a person?" Zaedi asked. "Could it be a creature we don't know about—one that strikes without warning and leaves no trace?"

Hangman studied his fingernails. "Maybe it is something like that. I don't know. We'll just have to see—but I think other bands and other Clans would have seen or at least heard of something like that if it was a creature. We would all have heard about it by now."

"Maybe it's something that only exists in one place—like the Anglers," Zaedi suggested. "Maybe that's why no one has heard of it—because it only exists here."

"No one had heard of the Anglers because they were trapped in that valley. They couldn't get out. Everyone would have known about them if they could." Hangman looked away and wound up staring across the camp again. "I think it's a person. Only a person could do something like this and get away with it without getting caught."

Zaedi frowned. "So will the person keep killing until they take out everyone in the whole band?"

"I doubt it. The killer wants to accomplish something. It looks an awful lot to me like the killer is out for some kind of revenge against these men for kidnapping these women and holding them as captives all this time. That's what I think."

"So...." Now Zaedi was the one who looked across the camp at the women working over there. "So you think it's one of the captive women?"

"I'm saying the killer has a reason to hate these men. The killer wants to get rid of them for that reason. The killer has no reason to go after children like you."

"I wasn't worried about myself!" Zaedi fired back a little too vehemently.

Hangman couldn't even smile at his son. Hangman took some dried food out of his bag and handed it over. "Eat your food and don't concern yourself with the affairs of adults."

"It's my affair if something happens to you or Mother. Then I would be responsible for Thena and Maeno. You and Mother always say so."

Hangman did smile at that. He outright laughed about it. "All right, my son. You can concern yourself with it."

Zaedi didn't pick up the thread of conversation, thank the stars. Hangman didn't want to talk about it. He didn't want to think about it.

He became acutely aware of all of Mora's movements down to the smallest detail. She helped the women for a while and then lowered a stone into the embers to heat a rock to brew Gooji juice.

Hangman's hand automatically went to his face. His scar didn't feel hot or puffy. It hadn't bothered him for months. None of his old Angler injuries bothered him.

Was she making Gooji juice for her arm? She better not start having problems with it after all this time.

He watched her make the juice and set it aside to cool. She came back to check on the children. Then she returned to the fire, tested the juice, and poured it into a bowl for Rivila to drink. Hangman didn't ask what the juice was for.

He made a strategic decision not to sleep with his arms around Mora that night. Everyone woke up silent and jumpy when they discovered Hook gone the next morning.

Blaze growled at everyone to move out. He didn't even wait to search for Hook. Blaze said they were too close to the other band and had to catch up with them before the party lost any more men.

He pretended not to notice when Coal vanished right after the party left camp. Blaze turned around once, saw the empty place where Coal should have been, and kept right on walking. That left nine men including Hangman.

He kept Mora in sight all day that time, too. She must have been sneaking out under cover of darkness and laying her traps along the band's route. Rust vanished right out from under everyone's noses during that march.

Blaze posted his remaining men in a guarding formation around the women and children at the center of their group. Everyone did it that way, but now the women and children outnumbered the men.

Blaze rotated his men into different positions. Rust had been in the front all morning. He vanished after Blaze rotated him to the back where the band couldn't keep an eye on him.

Hangman hadn't been watching Rust when he disappeared. Hangman didn't see how it happened.

It didn't really matter anymore. The others kept vanishing until only four men remained: Blaze and three others named Decay, Squash, Vacant.

They were the weakest, least alert, and the laziest of the whole band. That's why they had survived. They never left camp unless they had to and they didn't take risks.

Hangman couldn't tell if Mora had planned it this way or if it had just worked out that her traps took the strongest men first. Hangman could have taken out these four by himself.

He wouldn't have to because he had Mora. He even considered getting the other women to help him, but he decided against it. It would work better if he and Mora carried out her original campaign in the same way.

Chapter 31

B laze didn't tell the band to move out again nor did he wait around for the silent killer to make anyone else disappear. He called the remaining men to him as soon as the women sat down and started making camp for the night.

Hangman, Decay, Squash, and Vacant gathered around Blaze. He kept his voice low like he wanted to stop the killer from overhearing him. Blaze's eyes darted everywhere. He hardly ever made eye contact with his men anymore.

"We can't continue like this," he choked. "We'll leave the women here and go together to meet up with the other Kral. The killer won't be able to strike as long as we keep together."

"The killer has been able to strike when we've been all together so far," Vacant pointed out. "Half our men disappeared when we were all together. How do you explain that?"

"I don't explain it. I don't know what happened and I don't care. We just have to find the other Kral and get him to take us in. We can't wait anymore."

"Take us in?" Squash asked. "So you don't want to raid him?"

"We can't raid him with so few men," Blaze replied. "We're in more danger out here than we would be with him. He can offer us protection."

"So we would take this curse to another band?" Vacant countered. "We shouldn't make ourselves a burden on them. That wouldn't be right."

"Since when do you care about doing what's right?" Decay interjected.

"That's enough arguing," Blaze husked. "We have enough problems as it is. The other Kral can help us either way. We can't stay out here on our own. We can't protect ourselves from any of this. We couldn't protect ourselves from a Crusher if it attacked right now."

"We won't be able to protect ourselves from the killer if we take him with us to the new band," Vacant pointed out. "He would strike within the band and kill us anyway."

"This is a punishment for all the things we've been doing all these years," Decay murmured. "That's the curse. We cursed ourselves and now we're paying for it."

"It isn't a curse," Blaze snapped. "It's a person—but that doesn't matter. Let's go. We'll go to the Kral right now and ask him to show us mercy and hospitality. That's our only option at this point." He turned to Hangman. "You come, too. We have to stay together."

"Okay, I'm coming," Hangman replied. "Let me just go tell my wife where I'm going."

Hangman returned to Mora and the children. He squatted down next to her and told her Blaze's decision while he rummaged around in Zaedi's shoulder bag for something.

"Are you ready?" Hangman asked her in an undertone.

She pretended to fix something in Maeno's hair so she wouldn't look at Hangman. "Yes," she murmured back. "I'm ready."

He didn't stay long enough even to look at her or to ask what she was going to do or to wish her luck. He didn't even make eye contact with her before he returned to the men.

None of them had women they needed to check in with before they left. Blaze gave orders for the women and children to stay here and make camp while the men filed into the jungle on their way farther east along the river.

Hangman made a strategic decision to walk in the back of the group. He found his eyes darting over their route in search of any triggers that might set off Mora's traps.

She couldn't have laid traps here. The band had been too far away before this. She didn't have time to lay anything.

He had no clue what to expect from her. She would have to catch up with the men and maybe even get ahead of them. Then she and Hangman would have to attack and kill these men.

She wasn't the greatest fighter when it came to open confrontation. She just didn't have the strength or experience. She usually killed by crippling or weakening her prey so she didn't have to face it in direct combat.

She rarely if ever faced grown men in battle. She knew better. That was the whole point of using traps. Hangman might even wind up killing all four of them while she just distracted them.

He couldn't anticipate her. That was the most surreal part of this whole thing. She knew so much more than he did about this style of fighting. Zaedi had given Hangman the briefest sketch of what she might be capable of.

He would have preferred to know ahead of time what she planned to do, but it was too late now.

Blaze wound his way down the river going eastward the same as always. He took the lead by walking in front of the other men. It didn't occur to him that walking in front might put him in danger.

He also didn't seem to realize that walking single file might put the men in more danger than walking in a cluster. He didn't appear to think much in terms of how best to protect himself and his men from the killer.

He didn't tell them to walk in a cluster with their weapons drawn and facing outward for any kind of attack or threat. That's what Hangman would have done.

He heard a rustle in the treetops above the group. He looked up just in time to see a tall sapling bowing its head to the ground.

The other men looked up at the sound, too. They didn't have time to see Mora clinging to the branches and riding the tree to the ground. Only Hangman saw that because a Krakelow dropped from another tree at exactly that moment.

It landed right on top of Vacant in the center of the group. Hangman barely leapt away in time. He wouldn't have if he hadn't been expecting Mora to attack somewhere along this route.

She didn't have time to lay a trap for the men, but she struck in exactly same way. She had tied a long rope to the sapling. She bowed it low enough to the ground to toss a noose over Blaze's head.

He spun around to face the Krakelow—and then the sapling snapped back up into its original place. The noose zinged around his neck and yanked him off the ground so fast he never knew what hit him.

The Krakelow enveloped Vacant in a heartbeat and threw its coils around Decay and Squash to pull them in. Hangman leapt ten feet away from them and barely dodged one of the Krakelow's segments flying toward his face.

He hacked it away with his kukri. Squash and Decay got trapped there. They fought back and might have escaped in the end.

Hangman dove in, sprinted behind Decay, and Hangman chopped his kukri across the back of Decay's skull. Hangman didn't kill him. He didn't have to.

Decay when down under the Krakelow's coils. Squash saw Hangman's attack and spun around to confront him even as the Krakelow started to wrap its coils around Squash's legs.

Squash raised his axe to fight Hangman—until Mora came out of nowhere and hacked her blade against the side of Smash's neck from behind. He went down under the Krakelow, too.

Hangman pulled Mora to a safe distance and they both watched the Krakelow consume the three men. Blaze swung from his rope at the top of the sapling's crown. The band was gone—all except the women and children.

"Are you all right?" she asked him.

"I'm fine. Are you?"

She nodded up at him. "What do you want to do next?"

"You go back alone and explain this to the women and children. Tell them what you did and that I'm going to take them forward to the other band. I'll go talk to the Kral now and ask him to take us. If he doesn't, we'll see about meeting up with Shadow's band somewhere else—or we'll return to the eastern gorges and stay there. We can't travel with a bunch of women and children and only one man to guard them all. We don't need to feed these men to the ants before we leave. The Krakelow will eat these three. It won't leave any trace for the women to find—and we might as well leave Blaze where he is. No one will see him. The creatures will find him soon enough and then there won't be anything for anyone to see."

She nodded. "Go on, then. I'll see you later."

She walked away. He found himself lingering there to watch the Krakelow obliterate the last three men. Nineteen men—dead. She killed all but one of them.

Hangman finally shook his head in amazement and headed off down the river. He decided not to tell anyone about this, either. Another Godless band might not appreciate his admiration for someone doing things the Follower way.

He followed the river for five miles downstream to the east and had to climb a hill to see the terrain in front of him. He stopped there when he saw the river join up with two others.

A large band camped on the flats adjacent to the confluence. This band used tree branches and leaf thatch to build large, four-sided shelters. Smoke billowed from cooking fires between the houses. It was a Godless band.

Women and children went down to the river and squatted there to get water. Hangman spotted three men coming out of the jungle from the north. They carried massive haunches of Gorlock meat on their shoulders.

They delivered the meat to the women and then the men went down to the river to wash the blood off their arms and bodies.

Hangman's chest tightened at the sight of Godless people. These were real Godless. Their children ran around playing. Voices bubbled out of the distance mixed with laughter from both men and women.

These people behaved so differently from Blaze's band. Hangman would have known there was something wrong with Blaze's band even if Blaze hadn't spun Hangman that insulting story about Hammer.

Hangman took a deep breath and walked down the hill getting closer to the band. He made sure to keep his hands away from his weapons.

A bunch of men stood up and came toward him when he got near enough. Then the women and children stopped what they were doing.

Hangman had to fight down rising emotion when he got near enough to recognize some of these people. Viking, Red, Wildling, Butch, Legend, and Bantam lined up in front of him. Their eyes widened when they recognized him, too.

Viking broke out of line and charged Hangman, attacked him, and grabbed him in a huge hug. Viking burst out in roaring laughter and pushed Hangman back to search him through tears.

Viking kept bursting out in laughter. "You're here! You're alive!"

The rest of the men surrounded Hangman all talking and touching him at once. Viking wouldn't stop crushing Hangman's shoulders and shaking him. "Where are Mora and your children?" Viking demanded. "Don't tell me you're alone."

"I'm not. They're back there camped up the river. We met up with some other women and children. They were captives of another band and we rescued them." Hangman searched the faces of the men around him. He knew them all. They were his brothers. "Is my father still Kral?"

Viking got serious. "Yes. He is. He'll be so happy to see you."

Viking turned away to reenter the camp. Hangman followed him. Hangman didn't want anything to delay the confrontation between him and his father.

The women slowed him down when they realized who and what the men were making such a big deal about. All the women crowded around crying and making a bunch of noise.

It took a long time for Hangman to get through them all. In the end, Viking had to push the women away and tell them to stop staining Hangman with their tears.

Hangman did allow himself a few extra minutes to hug his mother. Viking pulled him away from her and led the way into the camp.

Viking kept glancing up at Hangman, bursting into grins, and struggling to hold back emotion on their way there.

Hangman didn't see where Viking was taking him until Viking led the way to one of the shelters to one side. Hangman didn't see anything special about it. That must be Shadow's house.

He came out before the two cousins got there. Shadow glanced toward the river to see what all the noise was about. Then he saw Viking leading Hangman toward him.

Shadow froze. Hangman couldn't read his father's expression. Was Shadow even happy to see Hangman back alive?

Hangman stopped in front of his father. Hangman couldn't think of anything to say. What could he say—that he'd found Mora and the children and only now just met back up with the band?

Shadow could use his authority to execute Hangman for disobeying a direct order from his Kral. Hangman had no idea what to expect even from his own father.

Shadow's mouth trembled for a second. He stared at Hangman in confusion for a minute like he didn't recognize his own son. Did Shadow think Hangman would never make it back alive?

Shadow stormed toward Hangman, grabbed him, and hugged him much harder and longer than Viking did. Hangman felt his father shaking.

Shadow kept rasping, "My son! My son!" in Hangman's ear.

Hangman couldn't make a sound. His throat ached. He put his arms around his father and shut his eyes. They had been at loggerheads for years before they got separated.

Everything was going to be okay now. Hangman could finally rest. He wasn't alone anymore.

Chapter 32

Mora raced up the river and approached the camp from that side to make it look like she had been down at the water's edge doing something else.

Rivila glanced up and then went back to work. "How long do you think it will take the men to talk to the other Kral?"

Mora stopped in the middle of the camp. All the women and children stood, sat, or squatted close enough to hear her. "The men are all gone," she announced.

Rivila's head shot up. "They're what?"

Mora squared her shoulders at all of them. "I'm the killer. I killed all those men. You're free now."

"You killed your own husband?!" Ruda gasped.

"No, of course not him!" Mora countered. "He went ahead to talk to the other band about taking us in. He's the last one left. I got rid of the others. I just finished off Blaze and the others a few minutes ago." She waved toward the river. "You can go down there and check if you want to. I can show you Blaze's body. I don't know if we'll find much of the other three."

Zona stared at Mora with huge eyes. "*You* did that? You killed....Fence and all the others....?"

"Yes, I did and I don't regret it for a minute," Mora snapped. "I would do exactly the same thing again. They would have killed my husband and my sons and kept me and my daughter as captives. Blaze planned to attack this other band—and I don't even have to ask what they've been doing to all of you this whole time. These men were the worst filth of the human race. They all deserved to die a hundred deaths just as bad or worse."

"How did you do all of this?" Ruda half-whispered.

"Never mind how I did it. The point is that they're dead and we're going to meet up with the other band as soon as Hangman returns. He'll either tell us that the other band agrees to take us in or we'll return to his father's territory in the gorges."

"We won't be able to protect ourselves," Chida pointed out. "One man isn't enough to defend us."

"Then you'll have to arm yourselves and prepare to defend yourselves and your children. I'm sure we can all agree that it wouldn't be worth keeping these men around just to defend us. Besides, it won't be a problem if the other band takes us. Here. Look. I have something here for all of you."

She went over to her children and dug around in their shoulder bags. She had stashed a bunch of other weapons from all the men she'd killed.

She didn't keep their enormous battle axes and stone kukris that would have been too big for her to even lift. Forget about fighting with them.

She had managed to keep a few different knives and smaller weapons. She had hidden them in her own bags and in her children's so no one would find out that she had them.

She passed the weapons out to the women and even some of the girls. She was just going through the group when she came face to face with the two boys— Shark's and Ruin's sons.

They were both about ten. They were the only boys in the camp. Mora didn't even know their names. They spent time with their fathers when the men returned to camp. The boys kept their distance from the captive women and girls the rest of the time.

Mora confronted the two boys. "You have a choice to make. You can come with us and cooperate. If you play your cards right, you can join this new band and you might just grow up to be good, strong, Godless men someday—real Godless men who honor their Clan and become an asset to their families and relatives. You can initiate into the Clan and go to the gathering when you come of age. You either do that and start following the law or you turn around right now and walk out there into the jungle to make your own way. I'm doing you a massive favor by giving you this choice. I could have killed both of you the same way I killed your fathers. That's exactly what I will do if you ever raise your hand against the Godless. Don't think I can't still kill you. I'll hit you when you least expect it and eliminate you. I won't give you another chance to change your minds. Make your choice right now and live with it. Don't look back. If you come over to the Godless, you have to give yourself to the Clan and forget about everything your fathers have been doing. Their way is wrong and it leads straight to the ants. Your fathers were traitors and they got what they deserved. Don't be like them."

The two boys exchanged glances and then faced her. "We'll come over with you," Shark's son replied.

Mora only nodded and waved them forward. "Come over here and sit down. We'll stay here until Hangman comes back."

She sat the two boys next to Zaedi and Thena. Mora didn't want to trust the two boys, but they were only children. At least she would be able to keep an eye on them if she kept them close to her family.

She wanted to be the first to know if either of the boys stepped out of line. She wouldn't hesitate if she saw either of them doing anything to copy their fathers' crimes.

She gave both boys food and they both thanked her as politely as she could have hoped. Maybe her comments convinced them to change their ways—not that they had been doing anything untoward before now.

She actually hadn't seen them doing anything at all. Their fathers didn't include the boys in hunting parties. The boys were too young to help kill, capture, or ravage anyone.

The camp settled down into its usual hum of evening activity. Everyone had better things to do than think about the boys anymore.

Mora made sure all her children got something to eat. Then she gathered her water skins to go refill them. She was just standing up when Hangman returned.

His arrival sent a shiver of tension through the group. He was the last man standing. The women probably would have thought he was the killer after all if Mora hadn't just told them the truth.

He glanced around at everyone. The women all stiffened and some of them stood up to confront him.

He crossed to where Mora waited for him. "How is it looking?" she asked.

He burst into a grin and then fought it under control. "It looks good. It's my father's band. He's waiting for us. They all are."

His voice cracked with barely restrained emotion when he said it. His features kept convulsing.

She grabbed him and hugged him once. "Is it, really? Are they all there?"

He nodded and looked away. "Let's get going. I want to camp with them tonight."

He went through the group telling all the women to pack up. "The other band is waiting for us. My father is their Kral. They won't harm you. We'll be safe with them. Come on. Let's go. No one will ever harm you again. These are honorable Godless. They don't believe in taking captives or mistreating women and children."

He rounded them all up. The two boys hung back, so Mora herded them in with her children. If the boys did behave themselves and join Shadow's band, then she had no reason to treat them any differently from the freed captives.

She made up her mind on that journey downriver to turn the boys over to Red and his men. They would deal with these boys and teach them everything they needed to know to become Godless.

Mora would be more than happy for these boys to grow up to be just like Red's men.

The party filed down the river and climbed over a hill. Shadow, Katha, Viking, and all the others came out to meet the band. Mora went from one person to another hugging everyone and exclaiming over everything that had happened to the family on their journey.

Then Shadow's band pulled everyone into camp. They sat down talking, eating, laughing, and telling stories late into the night. The long ordeal was finally over.

End of Book 5.

Keep Reading

Rise of the Giants Series: Book 6: Igniting the Flame

Kuvik's struggles to rebuild his life come crumbling down around his ears when he gets carried away from the Godless Clan by an Ashtaw stampede. Lost, unarmed, and retaken as a captive to the barbaric Bounty Hunter Clan, Kuvik's old demons return with a vengeance when he feels himself starting to slip back into the mindless servitude that kept him alive during the crushing ordeal of his early life.

Everyone wants to be Kuvik's friend and ally. Everyone wants to help him escape—but who amongst these strangers are really able to help him? Who are traitors in disguise and who are just too damaged to save? Is Kuvik one of those now? Has he just gone through too much heartbreaking torment even to save himself?

The journey across forever to reclaim his lost family and Clan will cost him everything, including all the most precious parts of his new life he isn't willing to lose. Is it worth it to keep trying? Will he ever find the people he loves and the life he thought he'd lost forever?

You can find it at your favorite book retailer.

Sign Up Once--Get all Theo Mann's free books including brand new releases

S ign Up Once--Get all Theo Mann's free books including brand new releases

In a world where everything is out to kill you, humans must fight for survival every day against huge dangerous creatures and enemy Clans. The Godless Clan has enough to worry about already. They don't need to fight their own.

Sixteen-year-old Shadow knows exactly what to do when he discovers a girl from an enemy band hiding in the jungle. He takes her captive as a prisoner of war, but the Godless have a strict code of honor when dealing with women—even enemy women.

He and Katha will have to fight for their very survival and overcome generations of mistrust before they make it back to their people—who just might be the most dangerous enemies either of them has ever faced.

Sign up at www.theomann.com to read it for free

About Theo Mann

I write 70 books per year—and yes, before you ask, all these books are my original creative work. Nothing written under my name is AI-generated or ghostwritten because I write better than AI and any ghostwriter out there.

People don't read fiction for entertainment or to escape from reality. People read fiction to see their humanity reflected in another person's character and story.

This is my promise to you. When you read my books, you'll see your own humanity reflected in the characters and stories. I take this commitment to my readers very seriously. My books are an intimate form of communication between us. I would never disrespect my readers by turning that over to a machine or another writer. This is my bond between me and you as my reader.

I write 20,000 words per day as my daily work output. If anyone with a public platform would like to challenge me to prove this in a controlled environment, feel free to contact me on this website's contact page.

I worked as a professional ghostwriter for fifteen years. Now I'm on a mission to set a Guinness World Record by writing 700 books over the next ten years and 1400 books over the next twenty years, all originally written by me. See my website for the full book list.

I'm also the author of *Proof for the Existence of God* and the *Crimes Against Fiction* blog. You can find all my nonfiction work at www.crimes-against-fiction.com.

If you have a story idea, or if you would like me to explore a series in more depth, or if you'd like me to explore a character by writing a spinoff series about that character or world, leave me a message on my website's contact page. I answer all reader emails, so ask me anything, tell me what you liked and didn't like, and let me know where you'd like your favorite series to go. I would love to hear your ideas and find out what you'd like to read next.

Find out more at www.theomann.com.

Also by Theo Mann (so far)